PURSUING MORGANA

PURSUING MORGANA

WITCH OF THE FEDERATION™ BOOK 03

MICHAEL ANDERLE

LMBPN Publishing
PMB 196, 2540 South Maryland Pkwy
Las Vegas, NV 89109

Version 1.00, November 2021
Previously Published as part of the megabook *Witch of the Federation*
ebook ISBN: 978-1-68500-573-3
Print ISBN: 978-1-68500-574-0

The NorAm Navy was primarily funded in its entirety by the Federation. Although each country had their own set of laws and rules, these were, in practical terms, more a façade to make the separate countries feel as if they still held a solid piece of their freedom within the Federation. Even the Federation seats were primarily held by Americans, but they always spoke of themselves as NorAm.

There were three main campuses for the NorAm-Federation Navy, with several other small institutions primarily in outlying areas near Canada and Mexico. The main headquarters was in Washington DC, the second, a recruiting and administrative outpost located near the very old Langley complex, and the third situated on Level 0 of the Meligorn-NorAm docking facilities.

The base in Langley was plain and no frills, with a few docking areas for spacecraft and the rest dedicated to airships and flying cars. The recruiter vehicles were mass-produced by the Federation Car Company—flying sedans with few extras— and most were dented or damaged from the careless traveling the recruiters did on a regular basis. These recruiters, though, were not given this duty station because it was primarily land-based or as a reward for successful missions. They were strategically chosen from the System based on test scores, comprehensive exams, and most importantly, the ability to speak with other people in a manner which was almost car salesman-like.

They were charged with the responsibility of enlisting the next generation of recruits for the navy. With its not always positive public persona, it could be challenging.

In one of the conference rooms at the Langley base, six recruiters sat around the table. Papers were strewn everywhere, coffee mugs half full, and notes scribbled and crossed out. These were the head recruiters, those who sent their subordinates out to get the job done. On occasion, they would go out themselves, but usually, it was only on matters handed down the chain of command with very specific instructions that required their personal attention.

On that day—and the several days leading up to that—they found themselves smack dab in the center of the busy season. School was ending, and the majority of kids within NorAm would decide on college loans, military enlistment, or the drudge of manual labor. The team first reviewed those who already showed an interest in the military. These had made the effort to go into one of the small-town recruitment offices and taken their tests.

Thompkins pushed herself back from the table and rubbed her face. "I feel like the masses that stream into the recruitment offices this time around are almost useless. Sure, we have more than enough morons to send out to deep space, but what about the rest of the positions? This is why I think the Federation needs to institute military academies in high school. Give those who are really interested the ability to spend their time working on shit that matters."

Holland, the man beside her, chuckled. "And they'll turn into the same bullshit they did two hundred years ago. Oh, little Bobby can't behave, throw him into military school. Then we have nothing more than a group of delinquents on their own for the first time. I'd rather take my chances on the idiot with no IQ who basically drools on himself but whose muscles are big."

Thompkins smirked and threw a pen at him. "You would think of the muscles."

He rolled his eyes. "Get serious here. Shit."

The other team members chuckled and the leader, Conrad, waved a stack of papers in the air. "Remember, we have already gone through these and made our choices. The remainder will be set aside to fill any last-minute sections we might have screwed the pooch on. They don't exactly like us too much down in the Gov-Subs. At least, the parents don't. So we won't get every single one of them, even though they already took the tests."

Taylor chewed on the end of his pen and balanced on the back two legs of his chair. "All right, so what's next then? We have the guys who already came to us."

Conrad put four stacks of paperwork down. "Right, so this time around, the powers that be want us to look into those who are already 'in world.' You know, the ones who have had a year of this and have practiced with the simulations and shit."

Thompkins leaned forward and curled her lip into a sneer. "Why would any of them give up their fancy-ass prep school education to come out here and serve the Federation? They are in the lap of luxury. Trust me, I was once there. I still don't know how I ended up here."

He chuckled. "That would be true if we were looking at those guys. But instead, we are looking at those who didn't make it past their freshman year. Those who washed out. Of course, we want to look at exactly why they washed out. We don't need any more Grants in this bitch."

Grant flung a piece of paper aside and glanced up. "Huh?"

"Yeah. Exactly." Conrad smirked. "We don't want anyone who can't cut it in the service, but we all know that prep schools are notorious for a hell of a lot of demands and little structure. It's not shocking that people fail right and left. We provide the structure they need."

Taylor bounced his pen in the air. "What about those three dudes at Pinnacle? You know, the ones who couldn't get past the Dreth ship mod but were hard working, relatively intelligent, and good with a gun?"

The team leader flipped the pack open and tapped on it in thought before he slid it over to Taylor. "Apparently, these fools went balls to the wall during the summer session and ended up passing the simulation. They technically made their sophomore stripes, so I doubt, after all that, any of them will chomp at the bit to sign up."

Thompkins grabbed the paper and looked down. "Really? They passed? I did not see that coming. They must have put their shit together fast to pass that sim. The last time they took it, according to our records, they lasted a whole twelve minutes, including the space flight time from one ship to another."

Conrad shrugged. "Yeah, well, I guess their parents lit a fire under their asses or something. The summer session ain't cheap, that's for damn sure."

Taylor pouted. "Pity that. We could have had some good raw meat."

Everyone chuckled, although no one had any clue as to what had really happened. They hadn't watched the simulation of the passing grade, nor would they. All they cared about was whether they passed or not. They obviously didn't know that Stephanie had been the one to help them through and earn their coveted pass—something they might have found interesting had they known—but nonetheless, the kids' files were simply thrown aside.

Brown flipped through the rest of that stack. "So, is there anyone in here worth looking at? Any beauty school dropouts who might make good on the front lines or anything?"

Conrad drummed his fingers on the tabletop. "There are a

few hopefuls in there, and one or two who have already taken the tests. We'll keep our eyes on them and see where they go. And maybe send some of the new guys out to talk to the others. They should be past the woe-is-me bullshit for failing by now. But remember, most of these kids went because it was expected, not because they actually needed to. Their mommies and daddies own half the private sector. It may be a waste of time."

The sixth guy, Chavez, came back into the room, carrying a box of donuts. He took two and plopped the container down in the center of the table. "It was like fighting wolves to get donuts this morning. Have we found the next captain? Next hero waiting in the wings?"

Thompkins snorted and reached for a donut. "About as hero as Taylor over here."

Taylor tilted his head at her. "Do you think you need that donut there, sweet teats?"

She put the donut on her napkin and chuckled before she swung wide with her leg and knocked his chair over. "Call me that again and I'll show you what these sweet teats do to your ability to have kids."

Conrad groaned. "Children, can we focus here? So, the other area was the Bank Test in the Games System on the Federation-wide pods. As you may remember, along with several other of our tests that we constantly have running, anyone can play them. It can be, at times, a good way to see if there are any diamonds in the rough—working factories by day and hard-core fighters in the pods at night to let off some steam."

Brown stood and wiped the powdered sugar from his chin. "So, I've spent my nights and days monitoring the system. I would say that eighty percent of the sessions started either never finish or do so after so much time has passed that it is almost impossible to see who the winner is. At any given time, the system runs over seven hundred games at once, depending on who jumps in the pods and at what time. Out of all that, we identified two possible teams."

Conrad flicked on the 3D screen which automatically dimmed the lights. "Team number one. They managed to deliver the robbers to the police department only twenty-two minutes after entering the simulation. Here is their footage."

They watched as the team used strategic moves to head through the different levels, teamwork to capture the robbers and keep them in their custody, and tactical weapons to power through the last set of hopefuls who sat and waited to intercept the robbers so they could claim the victory. When the replay ended, he went through each of the players, detailed their stats, where they were located, and any background that might be helpful.

Thompkins raised an eyebrow. "They're solid but they have no experience. Where did they learn this shit?"

Conrad pulled up the team leader. "Anthony Hammerstein. Twenty-three years old. Graduate of North Junction Prep School with a degree in tactical combat and a second in business. He said he liked the combat stuff. He was a poor kid from the subs and went back there to work for the family business."

Thompkins shook her head. "No one can ever escape that shit, even with a prep school education. Real shame. Real shame."

He flipped the footage. "Here is team number two. Note the completely different tactics."

The team watched them play and grimaced as they took heads off at every pass and used a grenade at the end to blow the gangs to chunks. Technically, they killed the cop too, but they got the robber into the cell. After that, they spent the next ten minutes congratulating themselves and doing dumb-ass dances over the dead avatar bodies.

Taylor chuckled. "As much as I like a smart-ass, considering I am one, these guys are douche bags."

Holland agreed. "We already have a cockiness problem in this branch, and it would only get worse if we searched them out. Those guys will get someone killed."

Thompkins raised her eyebrows and nodded. "I'm afraid I have to agree."

Brown made a slicing motion across his throat. "No good, bro, no good."

Grant swiped his hand like he used a sword. "All I want to know is why can't we have one of those swords out there fighting the Dreth? Take out some kneecaps. But yeah, no on those douche canoes. The slots for assholes in this military regime have been filled, mostly by the guys in this room. And you too, Thompkins."

She winked at him and grabbed her crotch before she looked at Conrad. "So, the first one's a yes."

Conrad pulled the files and laid them out in front of them. "Good. We'll get some guys to head out to…Missouri, Maine, Arkansas, and what's left of Texas to try to talk to those guys. I assume they all know each other, even if it's only in system chats. We'll offer them training as their team if they all sign up."

Brown grabbed another donut. "So, we get the specials from the recruiters, right? All the lower ones are simply spread out."

Conrad nodded. "Yeah. We take the special cases, those we think could be more than fodder, but we never really know for sure. I suppose it will be up to them once they get in. We can't force them to be good soldiers, but I tell you what, for some of them, the military life will be leaps and bounds above their lives in the trenches of these falling-down shitholes."

The other man shrugged. "As someone recruited from the shitholes of Detroit, I would have to agree. We have air conditioning, food whenever we want it, uniforms, friends, and ain't gotta pay a cent for it. Not to mention that the Federation's sad pathetic salary and benefits feel like striking it rich compared to scraping by in Gov-Subs, not knowing if assistance will show up or not. I definitely feel lucky."

Thompkins smiled at him and liked that he was so down to earth. "So, is that everyone? I feel like this week's round of picks is as weak as hell."

Conrad tapped his papers on the desk. "I swear it's the nuclear shit out there. Everyone seems to be even lower on the IQ trail this year—and that's not limited to the Federation Forces."

Taylor scoffed. "Because they know what happens. You go out and maybe you come back if you don't get eaten by some big-ass Dreth—"

Brown put up his hand. "Hold up. We missed one from the Bank Simulation. It looks like one person—alone—beat the test."

Everyone scoffed and shook their heads. "Yeah, right. That isn't even possible."

He grabbed the tablet and swiped over it to locate the footage and leaned back.

CHAPTER TWO

"Here you go, Miss Morgana," the school secretary said and gave her a wink as she passed her an envelope.

Stephanie smiled, took it, and held it against her chest until she was out of the office, down the hall, had pushed through droves of students who milled around their lockers before leaving for the day, and out the front doors. She headed down the steps and ducked around the corner to lean her back against the concrete of the staircase. Biting the inside of her lip, she stared at the envelope, hoping beyond hope that it said what she needed it to.

She stuck her finger under the edge of the flap and tore it open carefully to remove the page inside. There really was no reason to prolong the inevitable, so she read it quickly. Finally, she released a long, deep breath and smiled widely. She had passed all her exams with flying colors and as of right then, no longer had to attend the school anymore. It came as something of a relief when she glanced at the stairs and remembered that she had never actually stored anything in her locker. Honestly, she was thrilled to not have to go back in anytime soon.

"Hey, smarty pants," Becca yelled from the sidewalk where she stood beside Todd.

They both put their hands out and Becca laughed. "Are those your results? Are you finally out of this place or what?"

Stephanie grinned and tucked it in her bag, which she flung over her shoulder. She hurried down the sidewalk to where they stood and put one arm over Todd's shoulder and one over Becca's. "Let's just say that this girl is officially graduated from Chicago PS 34. Thank you very much!"

Becca rolled her hands over each other and shook her body as she made the sound of deep beats of music with her chest. Todd followed suit and broke out the "shopping cart," his extra special move for only the best of times. As he placed the imaginary cans in his imaginary cart, he bumped his hip into Becca's. "We knew you had it in the bag. But we also had some ominous dances picked out in case you had an aneurysm during the test or something."

Stephanie shook her head and blinked at them. "You guys are too much for one sidewalk. Seriously. I think people are starting to think you're having a seizure or something."

Becca put her arms out, her short, chubby frame always super-animated. "So, what's next, Einstein?"

"My new job, I suppose," she responded and couldn't resist a chuckle. "That's the whole reason I did this. To get there sooner. I mean, it's basically a life-changing kind of job."

Todd groaned. "While the rest of us suffer away in school, she'll be drinking champagne with admirals and lounging in her personalized pods."

Becca nodded astutely. "Personally, I think that you deserve every dang second of it. You have busted your butt for far too long. And after what Pinnacle did to you, screw that place. When my dad found out, he took them off the list of my possible schools. He wanted to show his solidarity."

Stephanie laughed. "I appreciate it. There are better schools than that for you anyway."

Her friend stood tall. "Why, thank you. Shall we begin your last walk home?"

Stephanie put one arm through Todd's and the other through Becca's. She was grateful that the girl's parents had once again relented and allowed her to walk home rather than be driven. While they didn't have too much longer left in school, it would be good for Todd to have company once she moved on, and he and Becca already had a good friendship.

He cleared his throat. "So, I came up with the perfect last-walk conversation for us to have. A culmination of all the walks, all the pop-culture, and all the times you were wrong."

She rolled her eyes. "Mm-hmm."

Todd rubbed his hands together and unlatched from her arm to turn and walk backward. "It's actually a whole bunch of questions but they are those that have never fully been answered. So, number one. Could Jack have fit on the door with Rose?"

"Yes," Stephanie shouted. "There have been recreations, there have been diagrams, everything. The girl was too prissy for her own good and she ended up letting her boyfriend die in the icy hell that was around them. Then, when someone came to save them, she simply let him go and sink to the bottom of the ocean. Personally, I think he should have sacrificed her."

He made a check mark in the air. "One we agree on. Okay, moving on. *Star Wars—A New Hope* or *The Empire Strikes Back?*"

Stephanie hissed. "Uh… I will go with *A New Hope.*"

Todd's mouth fell open. "What? Are you kidding me? *Empire Strikes Back* is when they completely turn the story upside down. It was the re-forging of the core rivalry between Skywalker and Vader with that arc between a father and a son! Tragedy came."

She shrugged. "Right, but *A New Hope* established the entire mythos of *Star Wars*. Seriously, every major player was introduced. The Force, the Empire, the Rebellion, everything while still leaving the door open."

"That's bull hockey." He shook his head. "You know that. Just because it set the stage doesn't make it the best one. How can you even think that the dramatic arc of father and son could come in second to *A New Hope?* Who even really knows that title? No one. You are no one."

Stephanie slapped him in the chest. "Calm down, crazy pants. Let me ask you this then, *Star Wars* or *Star Trek?*"

They both answered at the same time. Stephanie said *Trek*, Todd said *Wars* and they both looked at Becca, who watched them with wide eyes and excitement. "Hey, don't ask me. I'm only here for the drama of it all. I'm walking with so much nerdiness —will some sort of vortex open up and suck the whole world into it?"

The friends blinked at her and Todd smacked his hand into the other one. "*Star Wars* has action, adventure, Wookies, a storyline, and the ultimate villain."

Stephanie wrinkled her nose. "Right, but *Star Trek* is pure science fiction. The future. Yours is fantasy. I'm not saying there is anything wrong with fantasy but it's a cop-out to call it science fiction because it's not. And *Star Trek* has a storyline. In fact, it has about ten million storylines throughout history. From the books to the movies, there is something for everyone."

Todd gritted his teeth. "Not for me. Not unless there are lightsabers. What does *Trek* have anyway? Those beam-me-up-Scotty old-ass comms? No. You are absolutely wrong on this one. I'm sorry. You have failed me after all these years, and I cannot look you in the eye."

She poked him in the stomach and giggled. "I'm screwing with you. Of course I pick *Star Wars* over *Trek*. I wanted to see your response, that's all. It was about as wild as I thought it would be."

He clutched his chest dramatically and shook his head. "You

are a cow. I seriously thought that all this time, I had steered you down a dark and lonely road. Good Lord."

Becca giggled. "Oh. You know what we should do? Because it's your last walk? We should go get a shake at the diner. You said you would come eventually and it's your last shot."

Stephanie looked at Todd and nodded. "Heck, yeah. Let's do it. And they're on me this time."

He snickered. "Okay, rich girl. Can I even get whipped cream on mine?"

"Whoa, buddy." She laughed. "You are taking it too far…way too far. Psych, duh, you can get whipped cream. What is a shake without whipped cream?"

They turned right and headed to the small shopping area on the outskirts of the subs. Todd held the door for the girls to enter the diner, which was already crowded with students sitting around, laughing, and talking over shakes and fries. It had been years since Stephanie had been in there, but it still looked exactly the same to her—a long metal building with the words **The Diner** in sketchy neon lights out front. Inside, it was decorated in red and white, from floor to ceiling. The floors were checkered, the tables were red with silver edging, and everything had a sheen to it as if it had been polished for hours.

On the ViD screens hanging on the walls were old movies from the 1900s and early 2000s. Each one displayed a different movie with the words captioned below the picture. Overhead music played, this time from the 2050s but usually from about a hundred years before that. Stephanie assumed they at least tried to keep with the times before music was incredibly regulated by the Federation. Of course, that unfortunate time period was short-lived as people everywhere from rich to poor spoke out vociferously against the regulations. Music was the one thing that always somehow crossed the invisible divide.

The three friends chose one of the tables at the window and waited for the waitress to come over. She was in her seventies, at least, with bleached hair pulled back, a red dress that came down to her calves, and a white apron that matched the white tennis shoes on her feet. The varicose veins in her legs showed clearly through her barely opaque stockings. "What can I get you?"

Becca responded first. "I'll have a strawberry milkshake with whipped cream."

Todd tapped his fingers on his lips. "I'll have your split one—vanilla and chocolate with whipped cream please."

She looked at Stephanie. "And you?"

"Chocolate, whipped cream, and a large order of fries." She smiled a little smugly. It felt good to be able to splurge a teeny bit for once in her life.

The woman walked away, and Todd laughed. "Look at you, money bags. Springing for the spuds."

Stephanie shrugged and her gaze traveled the room as she soaked in the atmosphere. "Hey. Sometimes, you have to celebrate."

Becca rested her chin on her hands. "I can't believe this is it for you. We've all been in school with each other since we were tiny. Will you come back for graduation?"

She wrinkled her nose as she considered this. "Maybe. I don't know. It seems silly, though. Barely anyone comes back for it anymore, right? And I'll be in the middle of working. I don't know. We'll see. Right now, I simply want to enjoy my last day."

<hr>

The six lead recruiters sat silently in their chairs as they watched the playback of Stephanie in the bank robbery game. Their eyes all widened as she used magic to knock the robber unconscious and stepped forward. Ribbons of purple magic whirled around her and seemed to come directly from the floor. Her entire body was swathed from head to foot and her hair waved wildly. As she released the wave of magic, the recruiters bolted back in their chairs, their gazes glued to the bodies that disintegrated around her.

Almost nonchalantly, she grasped a handful of the robber's shirt and dragged him into the police precinct as if nothing had happened. All that was left in her wake were the ashes of the avatars she had taken out in the process. The video stopped and Brown shut it off. The team sat in stupefied silence, unsure of what to do or say at that point.

Taylor's feet dropped from the table and he straightened to roll his seat forward. "Okay. That was completely mind-blowing. How in the hell did she do magic like that?"

Conrad shook his head. "It is the Meligorn side of the docking station, which means it's within the MU spectrum, but humans aren't supposed to be able to throw magic, even there. And with the kind of control she had, she made it look like she could perform the exact kind of magic that she wanted to do."

Thompkins's mouth hung open. "Like she had complete control over it. As if she knew how to bring it up and send it back as a destructive power."

Holland waved his hands frantically as he squinted at the frozen image on the screen. "Hold up. Wait a second. That's the girl."

The others looked strangely at him. He pointed at Stephanie and pushed to his feet. "That's the girl who saved that woman and child from the runaway self-driven truck. Here on Earth, she used a battery to generate magical power. Her face was all over the news, but I didn't recognize her until the magic flowed through her."

Brown pressed a few buttons on his tablet and turned to the information screen at the front of the room. He brought up her pod number, location, and finally, her stats. "Stephanie Morgana. What do you know? It is her. She took to the bank vault to work her next piece of magic."

Conrad spun his finger lazily. "Okay, where is she? This is

something we cannot sleep on. If she is out there still and hasn't been picked up, she would be the perfect candidate. Our next hero in disguise."

The other man scanned through her records. "These aren't really updated because she just turned eighteen, but it says here she has the last half of her school year to go still. She is in the Gov-Subs in Chicago and attends the public school out there. She apparently did a summer session at Pinnacle but is back home now and continued her public-school enrollment when she got back."

The team leader thought about it for a second, then pointed at Thompkins. "I want you to find out who the closest recruiter to her is. I need them sent out immediately. Let's see if they can't persuade her that the real world needs her."

CHAPTER THREE

"I don't think I've ever seen someone get a brain freeze so badly that cold air blew out of their nose." Becca laughed loudly as the trio walked out of The Diner.

Todd chuckled. "I don't think I've ever felt my nose hairs freeze like that."

Stephanie grimaced. "That's so gross. But I'm glad you came out of it. I did not want to deliver you back home as a completely frozen statue. The one time we go out, you end up an ice cube. Your parents would not be happy."

He scoffed. "They wouldn't have even noticed. We don't talk a lot at home so they would have simply patted me on the frozen shoulder and told me to wear a sweatshirt if I was cold so they wouldn't have to turn the heat up."

Becca shook her head, her grin still wide. "Thank you for coming out, Steph. I'm really glad we had this chance. I know you leave soon for your big secretive job."

Stephanie hugged her tightly once they stopped on the edge of the town. "I will miss you. But I'll be back to visit soon, promise. And let me know when you'll be in town from school. I know you still have the rest of this semester here but it's off to prep school afterward, so I want to know you are doing well."

Her friend squeezed her hands and glanced at Todd, who still rubbed his tongue on the roof of his mouth. "I'll keep an eye on dummy over here too. Make sure he doesn't go licking glass windows."

"I appreciate that." Stephanie eyed him with real amusement.

She hugged the girl one last time and waved as Becca hurried off in the other direction toward her house. Stephanie tapped Todd on the shoulder and the two headed down through the subs. He finally released the pressure from his mouth and hooked his thumbs in his book bag. "It's gonna be weird not coming to get you in the morning."

Stephanie poked her bottom lip out. "I know it will be, but remember, it won't be for that long. Before you know it, you will graduate too. It will be a wild ride. And if it's that hard, you can always call me, and I can talk to you on the phone while you walk."

He groaned. "Oh please. I'm not that pathetic...okay, maybe turn your phone on in the morning just in case. You know, in case there are some bad guys trying to get me or something."

She kept a serious face for his benefit. "Mm-hmm...oh, sure. All the bad guys. Don't worry, dude, I will keep my phone on and answer it if I possibly can. I'm telling you, though. The first day might be weird but you'll get used to it really fast. It might save you a few minutes in the morning too."

They walked along in almost silence as they made their way through the subs. When they stopped outside her house, Stephanie wrapped her arms around him and squeezed him tightly. "Go home and relax."

"Yeah, right." Todd sneered. "I have to do homework like the rest of the plebes—minus you, of course."

Stephanie smirked. "Yeah. I have to pack, though. I haven't started yet and I know I have to take a fair amount back with me this time around. Not the most exciting thing to do, but it is what it is."

He gave her a hug again, turned, and whistled to himself as he strolled down the sidewalk. Up to that point, she had been fine, but for a small moment, she felt almost sad that all of it was over. Her life was changing, and the years she'd had to figure it all out were drawing to a close. She had to move forward and hope like hell she had made the best decision.

With a determined shrug, she headed to the door. As she reached for the handle, she paused when she heard her mom and dad inside through the open window. They hadn't noticed that she was back yet and were discussing business. Her mom sighed. "It's such a good opportunity. This could really fill that hole we've had every year and be a really good long-term thing. It could give us a chance to finally branch out, have a staff, and move forward with the company."

Her father sniffed. "True. Where is it again?"

"It's in New Downtown Chicago. Right in the heart—a huge skyscraper. The whole thing needs a possible cleaning service. It looks like 511 New Main Street—that really big one with the all-glass front and the multiple flying car docking stations along the sides of it."

Her father smacked his lips thoughtfully. "Well, we should put a bid in."

Cindy groaned. "I wish we could but it's in person only. I don't see how we could get away from the other jobs long enough to apply for it. Right now, it's only us and one part-time girl. We would basically have to be in two places at one time. But damn, that would be so good for the company."

Stephanie put her back to the door and retrieved her tablet. She put the address into the system and pulled the building up. Croftborrow Services was a leading player in the technological advances for the Federation. It wasn't a government building but a private business owner who, from the looks of it, had multiple

Federation contracts. Normally, that would scare her off but that was a good thing for her parents' company. If a corporation ran mostly off Federation Contracts, that meant the long-term money and stability would totally be there.

That was one thing she knew her family needed with their schedules. Stability. The business was so up and down that they never knew from month to month what contracts they would have, which was why they didn't have a staff. They couldn't promise hours every single week, much less pay for any benefits that might need to be offered.

She searched for the ad posting and finally found it. They needed a cleaning company willing to work the night shift for the entire place. They had a daytime, business-hours janitorial staff, but the night people would vacuum, dust, clean windows, empty trash cans, bathrooms…the whole nine yards. That would be a huge deal for her parents' company, and it would definitely fill their schedule. Stephanie bit the inside of her cheek and decided that she really wanted to help them get the gig, but she had to be sure that she wouldn't screw her job over either. She was supposed to return to Washington DC as soon as possible. But perhaps she could have a few more days to help them and set them up for success while she was gone.

After only a few moments' thought, she swiped over to her chat to see if Ms. Elizabeth was online. ONE R&D had set up a chat for the company, although only she and Ms. E were connected at that point. Apparently, it was highly secure and ran off part of the system. She wasn't quite sure how that worked but didn't intend to start analyzing it.

Stephanie: **Ms. Elizabeth, are you on?**

Elizabeth: **I am! Congrats on your tests. You scored in the top percentile for all of them. I was very impressed by your efforts.**

Stephanie smiled as she typed.

Stephanie: **Thanks! I was glad to see I did well on them. I** was actually writing to find out when you needed me there. I ask because there is something I would really like to do to set my parents up for success while I'm gone, but it might take a few days.

Elizabeth: **That's fine. Take the time you need. I can easily wait a week for you to get here. We had to purchase a new building after the fire and your pod won't arrive for another few days. You would end up hanging out in your hotel room anyway.**

Stephanie smirked: **You say that like it's not awesome. It's bigger than any apartment or house I've ever lived in. But cool. I will take care of what I need to do here and send you a message when I leave for DC.**

Elizabeth: **Sounds good. Have a good night. Celebrate. You have big things happening.**

Stephanie grinned cheesily as she slid her tablet into her backpack and found her keys. As soon as she walked in the door, her parents stopped talking about business and looked at her. She put her arms up in the air and twirled dramatically. "Well, it's official. I no longer have to go to class. I am all set up for success."

Her mom clapped and her father pumped his fist in the air. "We knew you would do it. When you said you were nervous for the tests, we both knew you shouldn't be at all."

She dropped her bag on the chair. "So, I was thinking. We should celebrate. I'll go up and change and I want you guys to as well. We'll go out on the town—all on me—and really enjoy the night together. If it weren't for the two of you, I would never have thought things like this could be possible, but you told me to keep learning and keep growing, no matter what. I want to celebrate that with you."

Her mother looked at her father and he winked at her. Turning to Stephanie, he smiled. "Normally, we would fight you on spending money, but I think it would be fantastic to go out on the town with you. To really get excited about the rest of your life. We'll go change our clothes and you tell us when we will leave."

Stephanie clapped with real enthusiasm. "Yay! I'll call the car company right now. That should give us all about twenty minutes."

Her mother gasped and took off up the stairs and her dad laughed as he followed her up. "You lit the fire under this one, didn't you?"

Stephanie sent a message on her tablet to the limo company and hurried upstairs to get ready. She picked out a nice pair of black pants and a dressy tank top with a tie on the hem of it. Once she'd pushed her feet into her flats, she pulled her hair back and to the side and braided it quickly. She stared at herself in the mirror for several minutes, shocked at how much older she looked. Maybe it was knowing she was done with school, maybe it was the clothes, or maybe she could see more of herself than merely the outer layer.

The limo honked outside and brought her thoughts back to the present and she grabbed her clutch and headed downstairs. Her mom looked pretty in her blue calf-length dress and her dad appeared in a pair of khakis and a button-up shirt. "You guys clean up right nice."

He thrust his chest out and pretended to puff on a cigar. "Yass, Buffy. Can you fetch the fifty-year-old Scotch for me? It's right next to my wife's diamonds. Yes, that's right, a huge stack of diamonds."

Her mom snorted and shook her head and the three of them walked outside. Her mom gasped and almost stumbled when she saw the limo waiting. "They will think someone died. That's the only time you see a limo in the Gov-Subs."

Her father still sauntered jauntily and ashed his fake cigar. "Silly us. We forgot the Jag at the other house and had to take the limo."

Stephanie grinned and climbed in after them. The limo was

self-driving and she had it take them to the new part of Chicago. There was a Japanese restaurant there that Becca had told her about a couple of years before and she knew that her mother would love it. Since it wasn't a weekend, they didn't need reservations and were taken to their own seating area with a flat grill in the center of it. The chef came out and bowed to each of them, which made her mother giggle repeatedly.

She ordered the shrimp and her father ordered the combination. Stephanie went with shrimp too and asked for a round of drinks in the little tiki glasses they would get to take home at the end of the night. They laughed and applauded as the personal chef cooked their food to perfection on the flattop in front of them. Steam sizzled and he flipped and turned the food to provide an amazing show for the three of them.

When the food was done, they sat and ate and talked about how amazing the place was. Stephanie was really glad to see that they were having a good time. She hadn't ever seen them let loose in her life, and that was really important to her. It meant a lot that she knew they were happy, no matter what, and they deserved special things like that night. In fact, they deserved to live like that all the time. All she could keep telling herself was that hopefully, it would happen one day, even if she was the one who had to make it come true.

While they ate, oblivious to any of them, a large vehicle pulled up to the curb down the street from the restaurant. Two men stepped out from the shadows and walked up as the front passenger window rolled down slowly. They talked for several moments before they nodded and slipped back into the shadows.

Another man put his hands in his pocket and scrutinized the two men who hid in the alley. The SUV started again and accelerated. It took the next right turn and immediately parked on the street. They were waiting for Stephanie Morgana.

CHAPTER FOUR

Thompkins leaned her head back and groaned as she rolled her eyes. "This is not the night I thought I would have. Seriously, why is this so difficult to organize? And why the hell don't we have someone whose job it is to do so?"

Brown laughed. "Hey, everyone, Thompkins over here forgot that she is in the Federation Navy. For a second, it sounded like she thought she was part of some big private corporation where everything isn't thrust on one person's shoulders."

Taylor rubbed his face. "Six people. Everything is thrust on six people's shoulders. And I'm not sure why it's surprising. Every year, we walk in here thinking it will be simple, and every year, we still sit here at nine at night trying to determine who will go where."

Conrad smiled and paused from taking his notes. "It's strategy, my friends. We can't send the wrong person to do the job. That's how you end up with low entry numbers after the busy season. We have to match personalities as best we can."

Thompkins shook her thumb at Grant. "Just send him. They will see that you can basically be brain dead and still climb the ladder. Or Holland, who will talk them to death, and they'll sign the dotted line simply to get him to shut the hell up."

Grant flipped her off. "Just because you think you're smart doesn't mean you actually are. If we all flashed our cleavage around to every eligible sailor, we might get promoted up the ranks quickly too."

Holland snickered and she gave him a nasty look. "How come I can beat on you without a single word as to how you look but you imbeciles can't think of anything that isn't sexist to hit me back with? It's really kind of pathetic."

Conrad stretched his arms above his head and yawned. "All right, guys, let's keep going before you bite each other's heads off, shall we? We have to send our best recruiter to the girl in the game—Stephanie Morgana. We need this one to be taken care of ASAP."

Thompkins narrowed her eyes and peered at the screen. "Let's see…hot, smart girl… It definitely means that Larry can't take it."

Holland tilted his head to the side in thought. "Remember, we only have Larry, Williamson, Charlie, and Rebecca who are qualified for special assignments like this."

She nodded. "Yep, and Larry will end up busting one on her before he can even say hello."

The man in question stuck his head around the corner. "Did someone call me?"

The six of them looked up and tried desperately to hide a laugh. Larry was huge with muscles from head to toe. While probably the width of three Thompkins, he was not the brightest crayon in the box. She pressed her lips together and made a slight snorting noise. "No, Larry dear. You can go back to lifting weights and saying the alphabet."

He blinked at them and nodded before he disappeared around the corner. Conrad's eyes widened and he shook his head. "Right, then. Not Larry, for damn sure."

Grant ran his finger down the list. "Charlie is out too. He is ready to leave on assignment for the science kid. The one who can figure out the chemical composition of basically anything and then make a bomb from it."

Conrad nodded. "So we either send Rebecca, where we could see how gender might play a role here…"

Thompkins giggled. "Or we send David 'Killer Casanova' Williamson. So, are we looking at whether to respect her with a strong female role or impress her with a hot guy with a good ass? I say go with Casanova. She's young and impressionable."

Grant check-marked the air. "Agreed."

The team leader shook his head. "I hope you kiddies are right. She's a must-have. All right, David it is. Now, who do we send for the guy who can bench press twice his weight?"

Thompkins threw her hand up in the air in dramatic resignation. "I got this one, boss."

Stephanie's dad took the last bit of steak from his plate, put it in his mouth, and savored every morsel. "This has been a fantastic surprise. I don't know if we've had steak in years. Maybe on our wedding anniversary several years ago."

Her mother nodded. "Yes, but nowhere even close to the quality that this one was. I stole some from your father's plate."

Stephanie laughed. "I think if I eat anything else, I might burst. Now I understand why so many of the richies are…" She lowered her voice and cupped her hand. "Rotund."

Her dad patted his belly. "I would be if I were one. Screw that trying to impress people with abs of steel. Give me all the potatoes and don't skimp on the pasta either."

They all laughed. Stephanie smiled as the waiter placed the paid check and her card beside her. "So, when I walked up earlier,

I overheard the tail end of a conversation. Something about wanting to grow your business?"

Her mother glanced at her father, who shrugged. "When you own a business, who wouldn't want to grow it, right? You want to continue to get bigger, be able to hire more employees, maybe take the load off your own feet after a while. You try not to have a cap on how big you want to get when you are growing a company, you know? You want to always see it as a future that is unknown."

Stephanie nodded and pursed her lips. "So, if you had the opportunity, you would actually want to grow it?"

Her mother patted her lips with her napkin. "Sure. If it were the right opportunity and made sense to the business. Absolutely. But it has to be right."

Dad wiggled his eyebrows. "Why ya askin'? Are you gonna give up that fancy job of yours in the capital and come join the family business? Maybe make some investments and grow her globally?"

She laughed. "After all this time of you telling me to stay as far away as I can from the family business? I think not. I was only curious. Now that I'll be gone and you won't have that expense, I figured that would open up some time and opportunity for you."

Her mother pouted. "I'm gonna miss your face. I'd rather have that than a bigger business, but I'd rather have you successful and out on your own with a big fancy job than anything else. The mother's woes. We don't want you to leave but we can't have you stay. These richies have it good. They can have their kid work with them and take care of them when they are old and gray."

Stephanie filled out the receipt, left a tip, and put her card in her bag. As they stood, she laughed at her father, who said, "Oh, she's still gonna take care of us when we're old. Don't you think little smarty pants got out of that one."

She put her arm around his waist as they walked out. "I

thought something like a nice little cottage on Meligorn. Then you wouldn't have to deal with the humans, and everything is much prettier on their planet. And quiet. They like their quiet."

He rubbed his chin. "Hmm, I like that idea. I hear they don't have poor on that planet, either. Everyone is taken care of."

She chuckled. "True, although I haven't been there in reality so I can't tell you much. When I finally go, I'll scope out the best senior spots. You will be young compared to their seniors. They live to be three hundred and something."

Her mom turned with a laugh. "That means I'm only getting started. I'm a wee baby on Meligorn. Why haven't we moved there yet?"

The doors to the restaurant swung open and Stephanie, Mark, and Cindy came out. They laughed and walked close together. The sound of their pleasure was comfortable in the warm city air and people didn't pay any attention to them as they passed. For a moment, it was as if no one had even noticed that they were from the Gov-Subs. That they didn't have the newest clothes or most expensive jewelry. For a moment, everyone was simply there to have a good time.

The driverless limo doors opened slowly, and the AI welcomed the family. Behind them, without their knowledge, the two men crept out of the shadows with snarled lips and narrowed eyes. The mystery man walked slowly behind them, his face only visible when a shaft of moonlight cast between the buildings around him. In utter silence, he tipped his head forward and grasped one of the men around the mouth with one hand and around the waist with the other arm. His buddy was already a few feet in front of him and seemed too focused on the task ahead to notice what had happened.

The mystery man spun his captive and slammed him into the brick wall. "Who are you?"

The criminal narrowed his eyes and twisted in an attempt to reach a knife sheathed on his side. The stranger caught the movement and snatched the knife from his groping fingers. He ran the blade along the crook's cheek. Blood trickled down his pale skin and he grunted at the pain. Finally, when it became apparent that his captive had no intention to divulge any information, the unknown man threw the knife aside and drew his hand back. He punched the thug as hard as he could across the jaw and released the weight of his body as the man's eyes rolled back. Gravity slumped him to the ground. The moon shifted behind the clouds and cast his sprawled figure into shadow.

Quickly, he turned to pursue the other assailant but stopped when he saw that this one was down too. His eyes widened and he fumbled for his phone as he looked all around him. He didn't have a partner and there had been no second person sent out to help protect her that he knew of. A little nonplussed, he stepped hastily back into the shadows and waited as the family entered the limo and the doors shut slowly behind them. A few moments later, the car pulled away and set off back toward the Gov-Subs.

"Shit!" he hissed as he snatched a key out of his pocket and raced across the street.

He fell onto his bike and shoved his earpiece in before he yanked his helmet down over his face. Someone else had protected her and obviously watched her as closely, if not more so than he already was. While that was good for her, he wasn't necessarily sure it was good for everyone involved. She was important—quite possibly the most important human being in many, many years. And his job was to make sure that no one, good intentions or not, got in the way of her potential and between his boss and her. What he thought would be a relatively simple job had turned out to be more than a little interesting.

He turned the bike and revved it before he gunned the engine and hurtled down the street in the direction of the limo. "Call E."

The phone dialed and Elizabeth's face appeared in the corner of his shield. She looked at her nails, an eyebrow raised. "I hope you haven't called me with bad news because today, I do not need bad news."

"The girl and her family are safe," he replied. "I'm currently on my bike tracking her limo back to her parents' house. She took them out to dinner tonight in the new part of Chicago."

Elizabeth rolled her eyes. "Good Lord. I guess I can't be mad at her. It's not like she really understands how important she is. She doesn't know the danger she could be in. When she gets here, though, she will have a full rundown in hand-to-hand combat as well as all defensive strategies. We can't take any chances with this."

"There is something else," he said hesitantly. "I'm not the only one who is watching her. There were two guys there tonight, ready to snatch her. I eliminated one and by the time I was ready to take the other, someone else had gotten to him. I didn't see who it was and couldn't track them without losing her."

Elizabeth's gaze raised and her lips fell into a flat line. "And you're sure about that? He didn't simply trip over his own dumb feet and knock himself out?"

The man shook his head. "Not unless he also threw himself into the alley, unconscious."

She snarled her displeasure. "Damnit. This isn't good at all. It could be someone else who wants her safe so *they* can snatch her when it suits them. We need to get her here to Washington DC and in the pod as soon as we can. This shit gets more and more complicated by the day. And if we tell her what's up, she will only freak out and we run the risk of scaring her off completely."

"I agree," he replied, his tone deep and firm. "For now, I will pull double duty and stay on her at all times. I have the cameras set up around her house to keep track and I won't leave the premises. Let me know if you hear anything about who this could be. The last thing we need right now is danger from some asshole company that thinks they know what they are doing."

Elizabeth nodded. "Acknowledged. I'll keep you updated. Until then…" She pointed firmly at him. "Not out of your sight."

CHAPTER FIVE

Stephanie lay in her bed, turned on her side with her back to the door. Her mother cracked the door and whispered that she loved her, obviously assuming she was still asleep. She smiled and waited until her mom closed the door before she rolled onto her back and stared at the ceiling. Her parents rummaged around downstairs, fixing coffee, but they always tried to be quiet to not wake her. Even when she was a little girl and her grandmother used to live there, she could remember her mother tiptoeing around quietly. For some reason, it gave her a really warm feeling inside.

She pulled the covers up to her chin and tilted her head to the side to look out the window. It was early and the sun hadn't come up yet, but the sky had begun to lighten. She waited for them to leave for work before getting up as she had plans she wasn't ready to divulge just yet. What she didn't realize as she lay there in the warmth of her childhood bed, surrounded by the pictures pinned on the walls and her purple comforter her mother had sprung for when she was twelve, was how much she would miss that solace and safety.

Everything in her life had been to prepare her for this time. The moment in which she would make a choice and erupt into the world using the talents she had been given to forge a path for herself into the future. Was the choice she had made the one that would do it for her? She wished she could say so without a doubt, but after Pinnacle, she had become a little more cynical about the world. It wasn't that she didn't trust her choice in ONE R&D— she had to, at least partially, to uproot herself and move thousands of miles away from home. Everything was shiny and exciting when it was new. Everyone thought she was shiny and exciting when they first found out that she could work with magic. However, like it had with Pinnacle, she feared the excitement would quickly fade for ONE R&D in the same way.

Fear couldn't be an obstacle in her life, though, not anymore. She had grown up with fear. Fear of where they lived, fear of the Federation, fear of starvation, and fear that she would never see even a glimmer of a successful life. She could no longer allow that to plague her and had to push it away and move forward. In order to do that, though, she needed to make sure that her family was securely taken care of. She needed to know that she had done everything she could to stabilize them and help them reach their goals, just as they had done for her for so many years.

After about twenty minutes, the front door closed. Stephanie peeked carefully over the windowsill and watched the car drive down the road. She flung the covers off and stretched her arms above her head and pointed her toes. As she rolled out of bed, she looked at the digital display on the wall. She wasn't late but she didn't have time to dilly dally.

In her closet, she pushed back a couple of old pieces and brought out the outfit she had selected the night before. She pulled the dress up from the bottom, wiggling her body as she drew it over her hips and pushed her arms into the sleeves. It zipped snugly up the side and she smoothed her hands down the front of the stiff but comfortable fabric. It was one of her nicer dresses and the neckline sat low on her collar bone, straight across, and dipped halfway down her shoulder bones at the back. It hugged her curves enough to be feminine and give her shape but left enough room in the fabric to be professional. All the way along the bottom of the hem, a slight ruffle of fabric rested right below her knees.

She pulled on a pair of stockings and wrinkled her nose. *How do women wear these things every day?*

The outfit came to life when she slipped on her blue sling-back three-inch heels and she stood in front of the mirror, satisfied with the effect. "Hair. Must fix the hair."

Stephanie hurried into the bathroom, brushed her hair out, and pulled it straight back to the nape of her neck. She braided it tightly and secured the end before twisting it into a low braided bun with one small, deeply parted piece that cascaded down over the side of her face. She took a little extra time to apply her makeup, using a tutorial she'd found online—natural but noticeable at the same time. She was actually impressed that she could handle doing it like that. Makeup had never been her forte.

When she was completely ready to go, she sat and practiced crossing her legs to the side a few times before she studied the information on the building they would be cleaning. It was only fifteen years old—relatively new, even for New Chicago. Every story was surrounded by floor-to-ceiling windows, all floors on the first three levels were marble, and the rest were marbled tile. There was carpet in only two rooms in the entire building—the office suite at the top and the VP's office one floor below. Both required a special shampooer that she knew her parents had acquired not long before.

She wasn't really sure what her parents' reaction to all of this would be and had yet to tell them of her plan. It would be better to find the details out before they got their hopes up, which would help if they were turned down for the job. Not that Stephanie had any intention of allowing them to be turned down.

She had put in the time and effort to get things done and do it right the first time. This was something her dad had taught her when she was only a little girl.

Satisfied with her preparations, Stephanie gathered the papers on the desk into a neat pile. She retrieved her mother's briefcase from the closet. It had been a gift one year for her birthday and she only ever used it for business meetings. She had programmed all three of their thumbprints into the security latch so they could never be locked out of it. Stephanie set it up on the table, pressed her thumb to it, and allowed it to open fully before she placed her tablet and the stack of papers as well as a cheat sheet of notes within. Once she'd closed and locked it, she headed downstairs and poured the last cup of coffee they always left for her while she called for a taxi to go uptown.

Her stomach was all aflutter when she thought about the meeting she was about to walk into. For some reason, ONE R&D hadn't made her as nervous as this, but then again, this was for her family, not only for her. She would have to rely heavily on some of her training and her experience in the interview to get her through the first business-based negotiation that she had ever been in. She had been successful in Washington, but that was a personal negotiation, and this was a different arena—and there would doubtless be significant competition. While she'd seen her mom do them in the past, those were usually small and with a homeowner who paid little attention and merely signed on the dotted line. This, she imagined, would be a little more tedious considering it was such a large building and a substantial contracted price.

Stephanie closed her eyes and imagined herself in that room, surrounded by elites as she made the case for her parents' business. She had to keep her shoulders firm, hold her head high, and always sound confident in everything she said. Facts were really important, too, especially since they would pay attention to what she knew and didn't know. It wouldn't be a moment to simply pull things out of her ass.

As she took the last sip of coffee, the taxi pulled up outside and honked. It was a driverless cab, one of the newer ones that had the ability to fly as well. For this, though, she hoped it would keep its wheels on the ground. Chicago hadn't fully transitioned into the flying car lifestyle and their airways weren't what they were in other places. It was a slow march forward for the city after the devastation they'd suffered, but they made progress as they rebuilt and brought in new technology almost every day.

With a deep breath, she placed her cup in the sink, grabbed the briefcase and bag, and headed out. She locked the door behind her, bounced down the steps, and hastily adjusted her steps to accommodate for the somewhat unfamiliar shoes and avoid landing face-down on the sidewalk. She slid into the taxi and buckled her seatbelt. "Croftborrow Services building, please. 511 New Main Street."

The AI in the cab set the location. "Very good. Total price will be forty-two Federal credits due upon arrival. Accept or deny?"

Stephanie checked to make sure she had her card. "Accept. Thank you."

The taxi eased onto the road, but she had no idea that she was being tailed—or that she had been since she got back from Washington DC. The mystery man assigned by Elizabeth now protected her at every turn. He waited until she had moved a little way down the block before he started his motorcycle. "Replay intel from inside the cab."

"Croftborrow Services building, please. 511 New Main Street," her voice said in his helmet.

He accelerated after the cab, surprised by her destination and uncertain why she would even venture downtown at that time of day. It was not like her and not what he had expected. Although Elizabeth had told him she would stay there an extra few days in order to do something for her family. That was the only explanation he could think of, but the details of what it might involve were unclear.

Stephanie sat comfortably in the taxi, her briefcase on her lap, and stared out the window. She passed through the Gov-Subs and waved at Todd as he stumbled sleepily out of his house. He didn't see her, too busy messing with the bands on his wrists—most likely to attempt to get them to play one of his favorite anthems for walking to school. He swore everyone should have a theme song and it should play whenever they went somewhere or entered a room.

She chuckled quietly as they turned away from the subs and headed through the cookie cutter likenesses of the homes in the suburbs. All the sprinklers had come on at the same time, all the lawns were the perfect height, and all the doors were painted a deep shade of teal. Anyone would have thought that a strange choice for a front door, but the Federation's main color was a deep teal, so it seemed to indicate forced patriotism among the middle class.

They passed through the suburbs and out into New Chicago, where construction was constantly ongoing and the scenery of people changed from the average and normal to the high fashion and luxury of a city. She knew she looked almost drab and plain compared to the women there, but she was okay with that as long as it meant she didn't have to wear the color fuchsia on her body and sparkling blue on her eyelids. In her mind, she was classic, and what everyone else wore didn't much matter to her.

She slid her card into the reader in the taxi and stepped out the automatic doors. As it processed, she tugged down on her dress slightly before she replaced the card in her clutch, which she put under her arm. Her heart thudded a little as she gripped her briefcase in one hand and turned toward her destination. The building looked even more impressive in person than it did on the site, but she wouldn't allow herself to be intimidated, she decided, as she pushed into the lobby. As she clicked along the marble floor to the main desk, she smiled at the already busy secretary.

The woman finished her call and transferred it before she looked at the visitor with a mixture of curiosity and flattery. "How may I help you today?"

Stephanie slid a copy of the email across the desk. "I have an interview with the CEO for the services contract."

The women snickered. "I still think it's crazy that he is the one handling this. He has over two thousand employees, yet he is the deciding voice on who cleans the building at night."

<hr>

Elizabeth sat in her apartment with her feet up on the desk and the phone in front of her. As usual, when she talked to her boss, there was no face, only the ONE R&D symbol rotating in front of her. She poked her finger at it with a sigh. "This needs to be done but it needs to be done right."

BURT couldn't have agreed more. "I didn't put enough thought into the security of the place from the beginning. The whole thing must be significantly tighter than last time. I ran some data on the most secure civilian buildings in the country and I think I know what I would like to see."

She smirked and retrieved a piece of paper to take notes. "Whatcha thinking?"

He paused. "I liked your write-up for the security protocol for the people and the building. We will go with that, but I would like to add gun emplacements around the perimeter. I would also like the building to be far away from the city enough to have the look and feel of a country setting. I want off-grid power—which I can set up on my end as soon as the facility is secured—as well as underground bunkers that are comfortable and equipped for a longer stay in case of an emergency. They should also act as a safety hub for all who work within the company walls. Obviously, with that, you will need food for a year and all that type of stuff."

Elizabeth wrote each thing down and soon realized that the new security would rival Fort Knox by the time she was done with it. She liked that and hated the idea of having to worry about being at risk because of subpar security. There were too many other things to worry about.

BURT continued, "I would also like a room for her to stay on site and live comfortably. I will leave the needs of a young human woman up to you. On top of that, I would like an eight-person security detail as well as six others who can be utilized daily for rotations or protection in other sectors."

She continued to nod her head as she wrote everything down. "All of that sounds perfect. There is one thing, though, that I think you may have overlooked."

A moment of silence ensued in which he considered this. He seldom overlooked anything. It wasn't in his system capabilities. "What is that?"

Elizabeth chuckled. "People. And not the holographic kind like you had at the front desk, but living, breathing people. You need to have other bodies on site. Otherwise, it becomes obvious that Stephanie is the 'special one.'"

BURT computed the information. "You may be right. I didn't think about that part of it. I think I can cross-utilize this space, then, if we purchase the land we have on the top of the pile. It already has a compound of buildings within it so I can bring on some stock traders and business people to the other side of the compound. They are vital to this business and I think that having you able to be in constant contact with them will be best."

She blinked, caught by surprise with this unexpected development. "Me?"

"Yes," he replied without pause. "We discussed that you would probably be the one to get the other businesses off the ground and out of their current paper-only state. I have grown my holdings exponentially and will need you to work with these people to enable them to start running my businesses. We will be a conglomerate of sorts, at first, and dip our toes into many different things. It will all be to ultimately fund the different programs for people like Stephanie. If you open your tablet program, I have sent a small view of the holdings that I currently possess."

Elizabeth flipped her tablet on and swiped her hand to the share screen. BURT connected and she watched as line after line of holdings cascaded down the display in front of her. Her mouth dropped open slightly as she scrolled through. "This is only part of them?"

"Yes," BURT said. "About thirty percent, give or take half a percentage point. I did not send them all since I didn't want to overwhelm you."

She raised an eyebrow, scrolled through them once more, and mumbled, almost to herself, "You did not reach that goal, that's for sure. I'm definitely overwhelmed."

The different assets, purchases, land, and stocks left her reeling. "The size and breadth of your portfolio are more than a little intimidating. It has to be the largest I've ever seen."

BURT sent a little more information. "It is actually number seven in NorAm, and number twelve in the world."

Her voice sounded as incredulous as she felt. "How the hell do you keep all this in your head?"

He replied in an utterly serious tone. "I have a big head."

Elizabeth laughed but let it trickle away slowly at his lack of response in the humor department. She couldn't really tell if it was meant to be a joke or not. She often pictured a giant dome image in her head when talking to Burt and joked privately to herself that he might, after all, be an AI. Right now, though, the image seemed uncomfortably too close to real. "What about connectivity?" she asked hastily to avoid that particular black hole. "It has to be secure and I think her pod needs its own connection."

BURT was already on it. "I will handle all connectivity and ensure there are three different access points. One for the others, one for the main building, and one for the pod. Safety and security are high priority right now."

CHAPTER SIX

A guard had met her in the lobby and taken her up a private elevator to the top floor. The secretary showed her into the office and offered coffee or tea, which Stephanie declined. "Mr. Martelle will be with you in a moment."

She set her briefcase in the chair and walked to the window to stare out across New Chicago and the old one in the distance. It was both a beautiful and sad view at the same time. To see the destruction and remnants of the city in the distance was almost hard to comprehend. It looked like a backdrop for a movie.

The door opened behind her and she turned, her arms folded. A middle-aged man with salt-and-pepper hair, a very expensive suit, and a charming smile walked in. He looked surprised at first but didn't skip a beat before he extended his hand. "Miss Morgana, it's very good to meet you. Please, please, have a seat."

He stared at her as he tidied his desk and loosened his tie around his neck. "I have to admit, I'm impressed with the way you're dressed. You look very professional and very well put together. I almost thought I'd entered the wrong meeting when I walked in the door."

Stephanie gave him a polite smile. "Thank you. When you do

something, you do it right from the beginning—or at least that's what I've been taught my whole life."

His smile was pleasant. "Very nice. It's not often that I have a cleaning company with salespeople like yourself. Although, until recently, I didn't handle this account. I got fed up and felt that a strong hand was needed. People don't realize how much money goes out to cleaners every year. I've tried the cheaper bot options, but it is never the same and I pride myself on clean and organized."

Stephanie nodded, her legs crossed to the side. "Life is chaotic enough without adding dirt and clutter to the mix."

The corner of his mouth twitched upward. "Very true. And while I will enjoy your company, you have to know that this is mainly to rattle the chain of the present company. I don't like to take it this far, but I thought it might be necessary in this case. They have dropped the standard quality while servicing their other, newer clients. While I know there isn't a single company that could survive on only this building, the quality of service needs to stay at peak levels. Right now, I hope this little threat will encourage them to focus on me once again."

She chuckled and snapped her briefcase open. Mr. Martelle watched her carefully, but his eyes very obviously lingered where they shouldn't. Nonetheless, Stephanie did not allow him to see her take notice of this fact. She took her tablet out and placed it on the edge of his desk. Perfectly businesslike, she pressed a couple of buttons and projected her data into the air.

He sat back and examined the graphs and charts that floated like planets in front of his head and above his desk. Stephanie put her fingers together and pressed them to her lips. "Do you know what this is?"

Mr. Martelle shook his head. She nodded. "This is the profile for the company that presently cleans your building. It shows the percentage points for where you stand within the company's total of business for the greater Chicago area."

She stood and pointed her finger at a pie graph. "Now, if you squint your eyes really well, you will be able to see that your company is a tiny three percent of the cleaning services' total portfolio right now. To put that into perspective, that is down from eighteen percent only three years ago. That's a significant drop in priority for any company, wouldn't you think? I know that in this world, we can't expect to be fifty percent of a company's focus. That would be insane. The business would never make any money. But their lack of concern for the job quality has probably crept in from somewhere in this fifteen percent drop in importance within their corporate structure. I'm sure that when they landed the contract, it was a hallmark in their portfolio. Since then, your clout has allowed them to secure even more high-profile projects, and their thanks is a reduction in the quality of the services they provide."

He raised an eyebrow. "I wasn't aware we had become such a small part of their company portfolio. That would definitely tell me that there is a valid reason for concern."

Stephanie pursed her lips and shrugged. "Personally, Mr. Martelle, I don't know how you expect your three percent to wag the ninety-seven. Let's run some really simple numbers because they don't have to divulge their earnings thanks to the commerce privacy laws of 2112. So, let's say their total income is five hundred thousand dollars. If you calculate based on that, your contribution is fifteen thousand. You are a businessman, so you know that if you don't put the effort into a contract, you'll inevitably lose it. But if you don't have the hours needed, you'd need to consider your options. If someone told you that you would only lose three percent of your total business, what would you do? You would skate by until someone found out. But would you fight for those three percent?"

The man leaned back and crossed his legs. "I suppose it depends on how much it is three percent of, but no, probably not.

There are much greater things I can do with that time that will inevitably make me even more money."

Stephanie snapped her fingers and pointed at him. "So, you see, no matter how valuable a client you might have been, you currently comprise only a small percentage of their present plans. If you want to do something to rock the boat, it had better be something serious."

She could tell he was amused by her words but was still infuriated by the facts she'd presented. He raised an eyebrow and folded his arms. "Do you have a plan?"

Stephanie swiped the numbers away and her parents' business logo immediately replaced it. She smiled and stared him straight in the eyes. "I sure do. You fire them."

Mr. Martelle threw his head back and laughed. "And let my building fall into disarray?"

"Absolutely not." She shook her head decisively. "A building of such splendor and architectural genius, not to mention the décor…I would never think of such a thing. Give my company a one-year contract, and if we can't do the job, we're done. And to sweeten that deal, you have your leverage to allow a general call that invites the other company the opportunity to come and discuss matters. It doesn't have to be a circus, but you might find yourself in a much better position."

He leaned forward, his expression sharp. "Just like that?"

She chuckled. "Just like that. And to prove to you that I am absolutely serious about this, I will put up a ten-thousand credit guarantee that we will do the job and do it beyond expectation."

He scrutinized with narrowed eyes. "And if you fail?"

Stephanie held her finger up. "Not that there is a chance in hell of that, but if we were to fail and you were able to provide substantial proof of the failure, you get to keep the ten thousand credits. Clean and clear, no questions asked. But I can assure you that by the end of it, having my company as your cleaning crew will be so beneficial that you won't want to fire them for anything, not even the ten thousand credits."

It was obvious that her proposal had quickly caught his attention. He leaned forward and studied her in silence, almost as if he looked for that one thread that would unravel her. The one piece that would reveal the Gov-Subs slum beneath her polished exterior. Luckily for her, that was merely a mindset, and the one she was in at that moment was nothing but strength and power.

He flicked his wrist at her. "Is the company paying?"

She shook her head and pointed at herself. "Nope. This is me, personally. I will put a ten-thousand credit deposit into an escrow account with the correct directives to be executed after one year—either back to my account or happily delivered to you."

He frowned as he considered this. "Why would you do this? It is obvious this isn't your personal company. Why would you put that much up against something you have no control over?"

Stephanie chuckled. "I happen to believe in the owners that much. In fact, I have never believed more in anything else in my life."

Mr. Martelle sat there in silence for several minutes. He rubbed his chin and his stare moved from Stephanie to the logo floating above them. She was as nervous as hell, but she maintained a controlled and calm expression. She'd learned to never let her opponent see the fear in her eyes. And he was the opponent in that moment. The one who could approve the hiring process or tell her to get the hell out of his office and never come back. Either way, nothing would have been lost, except perhaps some of her pride.

Finally, when his prolonged stare began to make her a little uncomfortable, he shook his head and reached across the table to shake her hand. "You are quite the businesswoman, that is for sure. I thought, when I walked in here and saw you, that you would be a pushover and that all I was doing was wasting some time with a beautiful woman. I have to say, I was wrong. You have brains too. Give me an address to send the paperwork to. Your owners will have to agree on the terms. If you'd like, I can leave the ten thousand credits out of their part and have you sign your own."

She smirked. "No need. We are transparent in every business deal that we do together."

They both stood and he waved his hand expansively. "But assuming we can negotiate, I think you are right. I need to shock them more than this. Much more. I will get those papers over to you soon."

Stephanie put her tablet in her briefcase, closed it tightly, and tucked her clutch under her arm. Mr. Martelle walked her to the door and smiled. "It was refreshing doing business with someone who knows how to do it. Thank you for that. And if you ever need a job, you let me know. We could use some ball-busters around here."

Stephanie laughed. "Thanks, but I don't think this is really the kind of permanent work I'm after."

He shut the door behind her, and she smiled at the secretary, who gave her a wink. She headed to the elevator and took it to the bottom floor. It was a long, slow ride from top to bottom, but she reveled in the idea that she had given her parents a chance at a new gig. It wasn't only about winning. It was about how well she felt she'd handled herself while in the process of doing so. Still, the cringe came when she acknowledged that she had learned some of those skills at Pinnacle, and she still loathed the absolute thought of the place.

She had to push that out of her mind, though. The hard part was over. Now, she had to tell her parents that they might have a new client who would blow their business out of the water. The doors to the elevator opened and she stepped out and nodded at the receptionist. She walked briskly through the doors and gestured to a cab. Her smile broad, she hopped in the back seat and gave the address. It was time to head home to make the announcement.

Stephanie was almost bouncing up and down in her seat as they drove through the city, the suburbs, and into the subs. Even the gloomy old low-cost housing didn't look so bad that day. She knew her parents wouldn't be home for hours, but she would be there and ready for them when they arrived. Her mind already on that appealing prospect, she paid the SD taxi, thanked the AI awkwardly, and almost ran to the front door. She hurried inside and up the steps, kicked her shoes off, and lay face-down on the bed. After a moment, she rolled onto her back, kicked her feet, and squealed for a moment to get it out of her system.

When she calmed, she stood, changed into a pair of jeans and a T-shirt, and continued her packing. She was almost done with it but wanted to make sure she would have exactly what she needed. As she went through her old clothes, she discovered a pair of yoga pants and a sweatshirt that she used to wear all the time. She didn't want to get rid of everything and she knew that she would need a set of lazy wear for work. If she would go in and out of the pod and have to remove all her clothes—that thought still made her *cringe*—then she wanted to try to be as comfortable as she possibly could be while doing it.

Needless to say, she was not fond of the fact that she had to get naked every time she used it. "It's like the eggheads who designed this equipment don't have any idea of what a female would find embarrassing. Because sure, we all love to throw our clothes off in front of perfect strangers, get cold, and lie inside an egg unconscious to the world around us. It must have been a man who designed the damn thing."

Of course, even though she didn't know this, BURT had designed it. As was only to be expected, he had done it in a completely calculated and data-driven way with zero thought to modesty or embarrassment—two things he had no real understanding of. He meant no harm by it, of course, but nonetheless, he hadn't thought that one through at all.

She finished what she intended to pack that day and headed downstairs as the notification for the virtual mail went off. Excited, she hurried over and swiped right to confirm that a package waited for her parents. It was the paperwork from Martelle. With an eager smile, she put it through and waited impatiently as the documents printed out below. The front door opened and clicked closed and she knew her parents had returned home.

Stephanie grabbed the papers off the table and giggled, really excited to tell them. She only hoped they would be as excited as she was. With the papers held behind her back, she poked her head through the doorway. "Mom? Dad? I have something to tell you."

They both looked up happily, but her mother's expression immediately shifted to concern. That prompted her daughter to hurry forward and put her hand on her mother's arm. "No, no. Not bad. Sorry. I don't mean to scare you with these things. Nothing bad at all. In fact, I personally think that it's really exciting."

Her mother gave her a side glance. "What did you do?"

Stephanie smirked. "So, the other day when I was coming into the house, I overheard you talking about a project at the Cromwell building. You said that it could push you guys forward —grow your company and be really good money. But the problem was that you didn't have anyone to go to the meeting."

Cindy narrowed her eyes. "Okay…"

She pulled the papers out from behind her back and handed them to her mother. "So, I went and did it on my own. I used what I learned about business, sat down, presented some stats, and offered a deal. He said that he liked the offer in principle but he's sure there will be some sort of negotiation."

Her parents froze and their mouths dropped open as they

stared at the papers. Her father walked over to her, hauled her up onto her toes, and hugged her tightly. "This is really incredible. I can't believe you did something like this. I honestly didn't even know you knew how."

Stephanie rolled her eyes. "Yeah, I learned it at the prep school. Once it's learned, you can't really unlearn it. So, what do you think? Is that what you want for the company?" She plopped into a chair.

Cindy laughed and looked at Mark. "Of course it is, honey. It's more than we could have asked for. Obviously, we will have to do some negotiation, but we will definitely want this job. No question about it."

Mark rubbed his chin and stared off into the distance. "I wonder if I could clean the outside of the windows in a super-hero costume? We will have to invest in a serious supply of window cleaner."

They all laughed. Stephanie put her hands in her lap and nodded at the paper. "I have to get going in two days. So, work on the negotiations, and on my way out, I will drop it with Mr. Martelle. I told him we needed a couple of days on it. He is fine with that."

Cindy stood and hurried over to kiss her daughter on the cheek. "You are more than we could have ever asked for in a child. Thank you for this. Your father and I will get started on it immediately—right, Mark?"

He nodded wildly. 'Yeah, we will. I'll get the coffee brewing. This will take a while—not that we mind, even in the slightest."

CHAPTER SEVEN

Stephanie walked down the stairs dressed in comfortable smart pants with a relaxed fit, black slip-on shoes, and a plain white button-up shirt. She pulled her suitcase behind her and its wheels *whomped* down the steps. Under one arm, she held her purse, and in the other hand, the documents from her parents for the negotiations and completion of terms of the contract for cleaning the building. When she reached the bottom of the steps, her parents stood there, ready to say goodbye.

Her mother brushed her shoulders as she always did. "I don't know why you didn't send those over virtually. I don't know the last time I saw a printed document."

Stephanie smiled. "Archaic, I know, but this is an important one and I want him to take it from my hands. Besides, we have to use up that huge stash of paper Dad was given when that print shop closed down and still owed you money. You guys never use it, so I might as well indulge my printing fetish."

A horn blew outside, and her father picked her other suitcase up. "Well, come on, let's get you packed in the car and then your mother can cry rivers."

Cindy had already starting to tear up and she slapped her

husband on the arm as they walked outside. They loaded her luggage into the trunk and Stephanie set the envelope of papers into the back seat. She turned, took a deep breath, and held her arms out to her mother. The woman clutched her tightly and tried to hold the sobs back, then stepped back and dabbed a tissue to the corners of her eyes.

She held Stephanie's hands and sniffled. "You be safe out there. Watch where you are at night, never go without protection—"

Stephanie wrinkled her nose. "Mom!"

Her mother sighed. "I meant like mace or a battery or something along those lines."

She giggled and turned to her dad to hug him tightly. As she pressed her face against his chest, she drew in that warm, comforting scent she had always turned to. She could hear her mom gasp slightly and run back to the house, but her dad held her close and leaned down to talk in her ear. "Knock 'em dead out there, kiddo. Not literally, but figuratively. Unless, of course, the situation demands otherwise."

Stephanie laughed and pulled back. "You know it. But like I said before, there will be plenty of security and I will be working relatively alone the whole time. Things will be good and the first chance I have, I will come home and visit."

Her mother returned, carrying a book wrapped in a deep purple cloth. She unwrapped it carefully and the tome almost fell apart. "This is…it's…well, it was in the family for generations. I don't believe it, but…well…"

Her father put his arm around her shoulder and his nose pressed into the side of her head. "Sweetheart, you may not know all the stories, but you are a Morgana. Read that if you can and make up your own mind. Just know that you being a magic user might…might…have come up before in your family history. Or it's a bunch of bullshit." Her mom jabbed him in the side. "Oomph! Or, fancy horse manure…"

Stephanie smirked and traced her fingers tentatively over the torn and tattered cover. Her father shrugged. "Either way, if you can read it, know that there might be a reason for your abilities."

Carefully, her mother handed her the book and watched her closely as her gaze studied every inch of it. Stephanie gripped the thickest edge of the cover and opened it, using her body to shield it from the stiff breeze. Her father put one hand out to hold it so that it wouldn't rip off the spine. She paused, looked up and down the page, and turned it. Her gaze wandered across the next page.

Her mother exhaled a deep breath and put her hand to her chest. "See? I don't see anything either. Only blank pages. Maybe you're right, Mark. Maybe it was merely some silly story."

"Blank pages," Stephanie whispered to herself.

The ambassador's card.

The battery rubbed against the outside of her thigh from where it rested in her pocket. She pressed her fingers tentatively to the page. A small trace of magic whirled from her fingertips, but it was too minute for even her parents to notice.

When the world needs a Morgana, one will rise to the occasion. There they were—the words seemed as clear as if they were written on the inside of her eyelids. Plain as day.

She opened her eyes wide to find her parents standing there, staring at her. Her mother looked at the pages and back at her. "Do you see something we can't?"

Stephanie released a deep breath and chuckled but decided to keep her discovery a secret for now. "No. I like freaking you out a bit, that's all."

Her mother laughed, relieved, and her father smirked and nodded his head. "Let's get this wrapped up and in your bag. You need to get on the road. There is a TRAM to catch and you still need to go past the office building. With so much to do today, there is no reason to stand in the driveway and stare at a blank-paged book like a bunch of crazies."

She smiled and closed it, wrapped it up tightly once again, and placed it in her bag. As her parents moved around to the front, she swept her hand over it to provide it magical protection—or, at least, she hoped that was what she had accomplished. It seemed more and more, as each day passed, that when she looked for a specific spell, it would almost come to her without thought. She wasn't sure if that was a good sign or merely a normal thing but then again, she didn't really have anything to judge it against. Perhaps the book might help her in that way.

All smiles, she shut the trunk and moved forward to hug both her parents again before she clambered into the back of the car. Her father held tightly to her mother's shoulder as they waved, yelled their wishes for her to have good luck, and Cindy sobbed into her tissue. She smiled as the vehicle moved off, knowing she would be back but focused on her excitement for the future ahead of her. It could be somber, sure, but she wouldn't allow it to create any stress for her. Besides, she couldn't walk into the building looking miserable.

The car stopped outside the large, looming skyscraper and the door opened automatically for her. She stepped out with the envelope and walked into the large entryway. The same secretary stood behind the desk, this time with a more pleasant look on her face. "How can I help you today?"

Stephanie handed her the paperwork. "I wondered if Mr. Martelle was in. I wanted to hand these to him personally."

The woman grimaced. "I'm afraid he has been on site but not in his office. I can hand-deliver them for you if you would like. I am not sure if he will even be back in his office today."

Stephanie frowned and tapped on the desk. "Shoot. I guess I'll—"

"Ms. Morgana," a familiar voice shouted behind her.

She turned as Mr. Martelle walked toward her with another person beside him. Instantly, Stephanie flashed a smile and retrieved the envelope with a whispered thank you to the secretary. She winked at her as she turned. The two shook hands but the man beside him simply stood there and glowered in her general direction. Still, she kept her composure.

Stephanie put her hand out to the other man, but he dismissed her rudely with a flicker of fire in his eyes. "So, this is her. The woman who thinks she can come in and take what is rightfully ours."

She drew her hand back with a polite smile. "You must be Mr. Wesley. I assure you, there was nothing personal in my attempts. Only business, you see. Attempting to provide Mr. Martelle with the kind of service that he has come to expect."

He sneered and turned to the other man. Stephanie's phone vibrated in her pocket as he turned his back to exclude her from the conversation. She stood her ground, although she stepped to the side. "Some no-name two-bit business, please. Don't be a fool, Martelle. Okay, so we took our eyes off the ball a little. We can do better."

Stephanie was faintly worried by his pleading and the fact that they had more of a personal relationship than she had expected. Her phone buzzed in her hand again and she turned to the side to answer the call. No one paid attention to her at that point anyway.

"Hello," she answered and tried to keep the sound of Mr. Wesley's gruff tone out of the receiver.

"Stephanie! It is Brilgus, the ambassador's guard," the caller said jubilantly.

She smiled. "Oh, Brilgus, so good to hear from you. How are you?"

He chuckled. "Good, full of too many dinners, I suppose. I guess I should stop having those when I go with him."

Stephanie giggled and ignored the conversation beside her. "What can I do for you?"

"I called to see if you would be in town tonight. The ambassador would like to have dinner with you."

She smirked, turned a fraction, and talked a little more loudly. "Why, certainly. I'd love to have dinner with the ambassador. I've been dying to catch up since our last visit."

Mr. Martelle shifted his gaze toward her and raised his hand to his companion. He stared at her for a moment and she mouthed the words, "I'm sorry," with a huge grin on her face.

He snapped his head back toward the angry man. "Two-bit?"

Mr. Wesley fumed. "Yes! Two-bit, half a company, no real talent. No backing. Some slums from the other side of town—"

The other man pointed to the young woman who stood nearby and laughed at something her caller said. "Let me ask you this. Do your people come in here to speak to me—the owner of the company and the building—dressed to impress? When I saw her yesterday, I thought she was the wrong appointment, not some representative from a cleaning company."

Mr. Wesley furrowed his brow and glared at Stephanie as she shifted her gaze away from him as she talked. "What?"

Mr. Martelle folded his arms over his chest. "Do your people go to Washington DC to have dinner with ambassadors who have their people call you to set up the meeting?"

His companion gritted his teeth and pointed his finger accusingly. "Now you hold on one second. Since when did cleaning become something you needed clout to do? Besides, don't believe this schtick. I did that lame shit long before she was born. She's probably talking to her brother or mommy on the phone. You would be an idiot to think that someone like her is that important."

He scoffed and gestured dismissively, and Stephanie narrowed her eyes. "One moment, please, Brilgus. I apologize."

She covered the phone receiver, turned to him, and pursed her lips. "First of all, I walked in here with the utmost respect, professionalism, and manners. I dress this way because that, sir, is how you gain respect, no matter what the business you happen to be in. If cleaning floors and toilets are demeaning to you and you therefore choose to come in sloppily and with an attitude, that is your problem. Because in my eyes, after watching two people grow and build this very business all my life, I can tell you there is nothing to be ashamed of. I am sorry that your business acumen and politesse are lacking but do not take that out on me."

Mr. Wesley looked at her, slightly confused, and silently mouthed the word politesse. Stephanie rolled her eyes. "If I weren't on the phone with a gentleman, I would say it in words better suited to your understanding."

Mr. Martelle chuckled, stepped back, and watched it unfold. He rather enjoyed the sparring between them, and even more so the way in which the girl was able to articulate herself to leave Mr. Wesley in complete and utter confusion.

Her opponent shook his head and looked at Martelle as he spoke in a low tone. "She is a fraud. A hoax. She doesn't know any ambassador and she sure as hell isn't traveling to DC to meet up with one. If she is, it's for far more than dinner—"

Stephanie's mouth fell open in rage but before she could say anything, her phone buzzed in her hand. Brilgus had sent a text to get her attention. **Please put me on speaker.**

She smiled and cleared her throat. "The ambassador's security specialist would like to say something," she said as she put the phone on speaker.

Even though Brilgus was either human or half-human, he still spoke in a strong Meligornian accent and a deep booming voice when necessary. "This is Brilgus, lead security specialist to the great Ambassador of Meligorn. How dare you speak to this woman in such a manner? How have you lived for this long without recognizing the pre-eminent human witch who stands before you? Had you acted this way in any other time or situation, I would have watched her fry you for your insolence. Show your due respect." His tone changed to a calm voice. "Shall we say the car will pick you up at eight pm then?"

Stephanie snickered. "That sounds perfect. Thank you, Brilgus. I look forward to seeing you and the ambassador."

They hung up and she stuck her phone in her purse. Suddenly, Mr. Wesley lurched and completely lost it. "How dare you put some half-breed Meligornian on the phone telling me I need to respect you, woman? I am under no obligation, and to think you would have some witch involved in your—"

Stephanie gripped her battery lightly, thrust her hand into the air, and waved it in front of his face. *"Enough!"*

His mouth snapped shut and his lips sealed. His eyes widened and he touched his face, slightly panicked. She narrowed her eyes, stepped toward him, and scrutinized him with slow deliberation. "Now that I have your attention—"

He mumbled, backed up, and clawed at the space where his mouth used to be. She tilted her finger back and forth in front of his frightened eyes. "I don't appreciate the slurs you have thrown at my personage or that of my dear friends. Do you believe for a second that everyone is a conniving, lying, lower than a rat individual like yourself?"

As if unable to help himself, he roved his gaze over the lobby and finally nodded. Mr. Martelle leaned his head back and laughed so loudly that it echoed through the marble-covered room. "Nice way to get him to admit that about himself."

The man, confused, looked at Martelle, back at Stephanie, and began to shake his head violently back and forth. Stephanie retreated for a few steps and folded her arms when she stood beside the other man and stared at Mr. Wesley. She admired her handiwork and how quickly she was able to translate her wants into magic. "What would you have me do? I have only two hours to get to the TRAM. I can leave that—" She motioned to his missing mouth. "Or return him to his less than admirable prior condition and allow the two of you to have a discussion."

Mr. Martelle sighed heavily and shook his head. He lowered

his arm and shrugged. "Take it off, please. I guess I can't have him run around my complex like that and scare the clients."

Stephanie raised her hand and snapped her fingers to instantly return his mouth to him. He gasped and patted his fingers wildly over his lips. For several moments, he stood there speechless, and she began to think she had somehow accidentally affected his voice.

Finally, Mr. Wesley spoke. "Mr. Martelle, I—"

The other man shook his head and raised a hand to silence him. "I want to make something very, very clear to you, Wesley. This is my building. The people whom I invite into these walls are only welcomed after careful examination of character, manners, and class. Apparently, I missed you in that review. If you ever come into my establishment again in a manner as brazen and blatantly disrespectful as you did today, I will have you arrested by federal police. Do you understand?"

Mr. Wesley frowned, and his nostrils flared. "Yes."

Mr. Martelle brushed his hands off decisively. "Good, then. It's all settled. Now, if you wouldn't mind removing your useless ass from my building, I would be much obliged. If you have thought about your actions, brought them to a careful review in your mind, and understood your wrongdoing during the course of the next three years, then you may reapply when the contract has ended."

The ex-contractor huffed and stormed out of the building but made no effort to look at Stephanie again. Her companion chuckled and glanced at her. "My lunch plans just walked out in a huff. Would you care to have a quick lunch in the building's restaurant? We can have your luggage brought in and the car dismissed and call another once we've eaten. I'd like to have a chance to get to know the woman an ambassador from Meligorn calls for dinner reservations. I doubt any of my friends will have a better story than mine for at least a month."

Stephanie laughed. "That was a good one, wasn't it? Although

I apologize for the mouth thing. I got a tad carried away, I suppose."

Mr. Martelle scoffed. "Please. That was the best thing I have ever seen. He's had it coming for years."

He put his hand on her back and guided her toward the elevators. As they waited, Stephanie looked over at him with curiosity. "Mr. Martelle, did you say three years?"

"Yes," he admitted as they stepped into the elevator and the doors began to close. "He was being a very large ass."

CHAPTER EIGHT

This time, Stephanie was alone in her cabin in first class. That gave her the opportunity to put her feet up and she ordered a small dessert—there hadn't been time for one after lunch—and a soda, leaned back, and watched the scenery change rapidly outside her window. It was a much-needed moment to herself. A time when she could reflect on her thoughts, worry little, and even shut her eyes for a moment and rest. She had to adjust to the idea that she wasn't home because now, hers had become a place and circumstance where home was less defined by the four walls that surrounded her and more by her own comfort in herself.

Taking the job in Washington was fantastic and she hoped that it continued as a long-term thing, but she had learned very young, watching the ghettos burn on the outskirts of Old Chicago, that everything was temporary. Even life was temporary, an extraordinary understanding for someone of her age to have, she knew. Nonetheless, it was there. That didn't take away her questions and curiosity, but it was something that lingered forever in the back of her mind.

Her cool, bubbling grape soda was refreshing, and she pushed the tray aside and rubbed her stomach. She thought about bringing the book out, but her eyelids already tried to slam shut on her. Instead, she dumped the tray outside where they told her to leave it when she'd finished, locked her door with her palm signature, and found a blanket before she curled up in one of the reclining chairs. The trip wouldn't take that long, but she still had a few minutes of sleep she could sneak in before the craziness of her new life punched her in the chin.

It wasn't long before Stephanie nodded off, her head comfortably cushioned against the soft velour of the chair beneath her. Her dreams wandered to visions of Meligorn, the pond from her testing, and a wide teal field of flowing long grasses beneath the purple haze of the MU spectrum. She looked around her and paused when she realized she now wore a long white gown that dragged on the ground behind her. Over her shoulders was a purple cloak, the hood slightly perched on the top of her head.

The energy surged through her, and with every step that she took, it swirled around her bare feet. Up ahead in the grassy clearing, another person stood silently. But they were not Meligornian—at least by outward appearance. The woman stood turned away from her. Cascading ribbons of long brown hair, secured halfway with rows of tiny purple flowers, rolled gently over her back. She wore a similar robe but long and purple.

Stephanie took several steps toward her and tentatively stretched out her hand, the need to connect with her astonishingly powerful. As if she were a character in a horrible action movie, the woman's body tensed sharply, and her head turned to look at Stephanie. Her eyes glistened a bright purple and she opened her mouth to emit a low moan that fluttered across the waves of wind and directly at her. Stephanie backed away and raised her hand as the sound drew closer and billowed into a large cloud of magic. She screamed instinctively as the purple mass rolled inexorably toward her.

Confused and actually afraid, she lurched forward in the chair and clutched her chest, breathing heavily. A sound at the door made her jump, and she looked up to where one of the attendants knocked a second time. She straightened her shirt and hair and pushed to her feet, shuffled to the door, and pressed her palm against the device to open it.

"I'm sorry, ma'am. Your door was locked. We have arrived in Washington."

She turned toward the window and blinked at the bustling train station outside. The man seemed to want a response, so she looked at him and nodded. "Thank you."

He glanced at her bags. "Can I help you with those?"

Stephanie shook her head and pulled them down easily, still slightly dazed from sleep. "No, thank you. I've got them."

He stood to the side and smiled at her as she exited the train and stepped onto the sidewalk. The warm late evening air soothed her neck and the throbbing pulse of her muscles, stiff from the way she'd been lying. As she approached the curb, she found her car, waiting like before, and it took her quickly to the hotel.

She was in the same suite, and everyone fell over themselves in their efforts to welcome her. Despite her efforts to shake the strange fog of the dream from her brain, she struggled to do so. Safely in her suite, she sent her family a message that she had arrived and jumped in the shower. Like magic, the water ran over her and washed away the heaviness that had sat in her chest like a rock. A little more relaxed, she dried herself off thoroughly and looked at the time. She still had two hours before she would be picked up for dinner.

The balcony door was cracked to allow a small breeze to drift in. She walked outside and looked at the view. From there, she could see most of the major historical monuments—or the ruins of them, at least. To her right, about three blocks up, was a more active area where people laughed, wandered around, and shopped from vendors in the street. Music and voices drifted up toward her and carried what appeared to be a pleasant vibe. On impulse, she threw on a pair of shorts, a T-shirt, ball cap, and tennis shoes and headed out there.

For some reason, her body appeared so much more acute than before. All her senses seemed to be aroused. The place felt wild to her like it was another time or place. The skies were clearer there than in other places as they had used technology to clear the smog in Washington before they had bothered to do so anywhere else. But in place of banners, planes, or open views were a plethora of flying cars. An entire network of roads, streets, and intersections hung above the city. From down below, it didn't look like they drove any better in the sky then they did on the ground. But it cleared the streets up and made for a more comfortable walk around town.

All along the blocks, digital holograms—some small and others larger than people—floated in and out to advertise a shop or some product placement for tourists. Several times, Stephanie almost lost her way as she strolled through several stores in a row and sensed the small touch of electricity in them. She watched people, too, but her eyes reacted in a way that seemed unnatural to her as if she scanned everyone she saw. There was a level of suspicion in her chest, something that up until that point, she had not experienced.

She wanted to know who the people around her were, where they were going, and what they were up to behind closed doors. As she approached an intersection, eating some hot nuts casually from a brown paper bag, she glanced up in bemusement. Two guys and one girl stood on the other side of the road. They barely glanced at her and all wore black, shiny clothing, their hair wild and teased, and the guys had applied more black eyeliner than she had.

There was no real evidence other than their looks to give Stephanie a bad feeling, but for some reason, she felt that they could be dangerous. She looked at her watch and cursed as she threw the bag in the trash. As she hurried back the way she had come, she glanced around one last time but the three were nowhere to be seen. She shook off the odd wariness that had stirred in her at the sight of them and jogged back to her hotel where the doorman stood smiling. "Nice walk, ma'am?"

Stephanie nodded. "Yes. Thank you. I should have a guest pick me up here in thirty minutes. I am not sure if it is only a car or the Ambassador of Meligorn himself. Please call me if I am not back down here when they arrive."

The doorman looked a little thrown off by the name, but he recovered himself quickly. "Yes, of course. Let us know if you need anything."

"Thank you."

She jogged through the lobby, into her private elevator, and up to her suite. Thank goodness she had already taken a shower and laid out her clothes because otherwise, she would be up shit creek with an ambassador coming to see her. Her hand on the closet door, she waited for the light on the side to turn green before she opened it. She had set it to de-wrinkle her dress for the evening and it also scented it with a sweet mystical scent of Meligorn flowers.

The smell calmed her nerves instantly and she eased the dress over her head. It sat off the shoulders, but sleeveless, hugged the bust, and flared out slightly at the waist. The dark-blue fabric appeared to have stars sparkling through it. It was one of the most expensive pieces she had originally bought, but she hadn't been able to resist it. She slipped her flats on and turned her attention to her hair. The soft, wind-dried curls complemented the look well.

So, with a pat of powder, a dash of lipstick, and a pair of earrings her mother had given her, she was ready to go. In fact, she was so ready that she still had fifteen minutes to wait. In case they arrived early, she decided to head down and wait in the lobby. As soon as the doors opened, the concierge came to her with a smile. "Is there something we can do for you, Ms. Morgana?"

Stephanie tilted her head slightly and smiled. "No, thank you. I am actually waiting down here for my company this evening to pick me up. They won't be here for another ten minutes or so."

He raised an eyebrow and gestured to a passing waiter, who returned a few minutes later to place a glass of champagne on the countertop. "Just long enough to relax with a glass of champagne, still grown in Champagne. We are lucky to be able to travel there and bring several cases back a couple of times a year."

She was shocked. Even the richies didn't often have champagne due to the lack of trade between NorAm and the rest of the world. The land in most of the United States was far too soiled by nuclear waste and other disasters to grow anything even remotely like a grape. She closed her eyes and took a sip. The bitter beginning and sweet bubbly end tickled her senses.

She smiled her appreciation. "Thank you so much. This is such a nice treat."

The concierge placed his hands in front of him. "You are quite welcome, young lady. If I may be so bold to say so, many of us here very much look up to your achievements. We, as a staff, have spent most of our lives in the Washington, Virginia, or Maryland subs. To see someone break free of that stronghold and be one with magical abilities on top of that is a true princess story that keeps us hoping."

Stephanie was truly touched by this. "Oh…I'm sorry, I didn't get your name."

He tapped his nametag. "Mr. Holden, ma'am. But you may call me Rufus if you please."

The doorman cleared his throat and Rufus put his arm out. "Your carriage has arrived."

She handed him the glass. "Thank you. I will see you when I get back."

A chauffeur held the door open for her when she stepped out of the hotel. It was a self-driving vehicle, but he was there for more of a personal touch. A protection unit sat in both the front and back of the car, and Stephanie could only assume that the Ambassador himself would be present. The attendant took her hand and she stepped into the vehicle and scooted carefully into the seat. Sitting across from her were Brilgus and the ambassador.

Stephanie, having learned the seated greeting, put her hands together and bowed her head in reverence. As she raised it once more, she spoke. "H'lemish Monguild Brathius Shode."

The ambassador smiled and nodded. "And right back to you. Though I would say, it is pronounced *Shod*, without the long o. The other pronunciation is more what the Meligornians refer to as the…uhm…"

He looked at Brilgus, perplexed, who held his chuckle back. "Yes, of course. It is the anal sphincter of a human."

She covered her mouth and giggled. "Oh no. I just said, it is an honor and privilege, anal sphincter?"

Brilgus shook with his effort to hold back a laugh but the ambassador ignored his bodyguard and simply let it out. They all laughed then, which lightened the mood considerably. Stephanie wiped tears from under her eyes and fanned her face. "Oh…that was not how I imagined it in my head."

Her host chuckled again. "Don't worry. It is a common mistake and most humans are rarely corrected. A little Meligornian humor, I suppose. Although I wouldn't want you to meet anyone of importance and make the mistake."

Stephanie slid the tissue back in her clutch and glanced at him. "I appreciate it."

Brilgus shifted slightly and his enormous muscles ground into the corner. "You do very well, though. Better than almost any human I have spoken to."

The ambassador nodded his head. "Oh, yes. I would have to

say just as well, if not almost better, than the liaison I have at the moment."

The car came slowly to a stop and the chauffeur opened the door to let Brilgus out first, then Stephanie, and finally, the ambassador. They stood in front of one of the most exclusive restaurants in Washington, and all Stephanie could do was hold back giggles for calling the ambassador an asshole.

CHAPTER NINE

The room began to lighten slowly, and Stephanie yawned loudly as the chirping of birds lifted the mood. That morning, though, she wanted to hit the snooze button, if there even was one, and go back to bed. She had stayed at the restaurant with Brilgus and the ambassador until nearly one in the morning. They simply talked and laughed, and he had taught her so many words. She knew how to ask for food, how to ask how someone was, and how to talk about family and friends. She had never picked Spanish up like that in school, but Meligornian felt almost like it came naturally to her.

She hauled herself to the end of the bed and rubbed her face. "Sarah."

The AI responded. "Yes?"

"Could you order me some coffee and breakfast?" She yawned.

"I have already done so. As soon as you have finished your shower, it will be on the table," she replied, and the shower clicked on in the bathroom. "Shower set to a comfortable one hundred and seven degrees, your last known preference."

Stephanie pushed herself from the bed and shuffled into the

bathroom. Her eyes opened a little wider as the fragrance of menthol and eucalyptus awakened her senses. She showered and sat down at the breakfast table, sipped her coffee, and pulled at a croissant as she scanned through the news on the tabletop tablet to her right.

"More unrest in space with the Dreth, Sarah," she said with a sigh.

Sarah emitted an AI digital sigh. "Yes, I have heard that tensions are high between the Dreth and the Federation. They are fighting back harder."

Stephanie raised an eyebrow. "Did you sigh?"

"My programming has been updated to include other responses to make me feel more human."

She straightened quickly, intrigued. "Like what? Can you laugh?"

The AI paused. "Yes, a laugh is in the queue. Would you like to hear it?"

Stephanie put her croissant down and smiled. "Of course I would."

There was another slight pause and the AI began to laugh. Unfortunately, it sounded slightly like a sped-up recording of a child's laugh. Stephanie blinked and covered her ears. "Oh no. Oh, that was…your engineer should be ashamed."

"Was it bad?" Sarah asked.

She wiped her mouth and chuckled. "Close to what I would imagine the sound of a dozen hamsters caught in a blender would be. Can I disable the laugh?"

The AI responded, "Laugh disabled."

Stephanie dressed for the day and opted not for her most comfortable outfit but something that also wasn't fancy in the least. She decided that as this was her first day back, she would save the yoga pants for the second day. Downstairs, she was greeted by the concierge who showed her to the self-driven car that would take her to work.

"Rufus," Stephanie said and stared at the car. "Is this a flying car?"

He nodded. "Oh, yes. The newest and best."

She pursed her lips and nodded uncertainly as she stared at it. "I've never been in a flying car before. Much less a self-driving flying car."

Rufus walked over and opened the door. "Then may I suggest buckling up tight? It can often be somewhat turbulent up there. I prefer to steer my own, but since you haven't been trained, I would let it drive you to work this time around."

Stephanie dragged in a deep breath and patted him on the shoulder. "Right, then. I will add that to my training list. Until then, I hope it's clear skies."

It was clear skies but being up in the air in a tin can was not something she adapted too either quickly or easily. Stephanie essentially flew the entire way to the new building outside the city with her eyes clenched shut and her stomach lurching every time it dropped or rose to the various levels of the airway. It was exactly how she imagined the old rollercoasters that Todd was obsessed with would feel like.

The car descended slowly in front of the new building and a man walked out to open her door. She glanced at him for a second and he responded with a toothy grin. "Hi, I'm Lars. I'm one of your security team."

Stephanie pulled her bag out of the trunk, her chin lifted in surprise. "Oh? I didn't know I needed security."

He chuckled and held the door open for her. "I think as the only magical human on Earth, you might need a little someone watching your back from time to time, right?"

"I guess." Stephanie shrugged. "Why not? The more the merrier, right? Where do I find Ms. Elizabeth?"

She glanced around and realized she had no idea where she was. "And... I...where am I?"

Lars laughed, his dimples deep and his eyes a crystal-blue. "It's a new building, and things are far more secure and better maintained. Ms. E actually asked me to escort you to the pod room, where she said you would know what to do. And she said that when you are finished with that session, she will meet up with you. She had to finish a few things, but she said you would find a familiar voice inside."

Stephanie raised her eyebrow. "Oh, Lord. I hope they didn't make the AI sound like my mom or something."

Lars smirked as he led her down the freshly painted hallways —which boasted cameras in every corner—and sparkling tiled floors. He stopped in front of a large metal door and put his hand out. "Uh. Palm, then retina, and it opens from there. They have all this in the system from your first visit. Only three people have access—you, Ms. E, and me, but I only have it for an extreme emergency."

Stephanie turned and poked him in the chest. "No peeking. None."

He put his hands up. "I am always professional. Although Ms. E might not be if you don't get in there."

She turned and placed her palm on the pad, then jumped slightly as the retina scanner popped out in front of her. Lars gestured for her to place her chin in the strap and it scanned her eye before the door lock popped. She turned the big handle and walked in as the lights flickered on. The floor was covered with some sort of foam-like material and she bounced slightly as she walked.

When she glanced back at Lars, he nodded, closed the door, and turned the handle. The light above the door went from red to green and the ambient lighting dimmed slightly for comfort. She walked to a table in the corner and undressed, folded her things, and set them neatly on the table. Instinctively, she wrapped her arms around herself and shivered, narrowing her eyes up toward the ceiling as if she were inside the Virtual Realm, and gave her AI a virtual middle finger.

Stephanie climbed into the pod and closed the door. The shift into the other world was as seamless as before and when she opened her eyes, she stood in a large stone building. The sand beneath her feet was white and sparkling flecks shimmered through it despite the lack of natural light. She wore a long, flowing purple skirt and a tank top with flowers pinned down the back of her loose braid.

"Hello, Stephanie," a voice echoed.

She had heard that voice before. Delight rippled through her and she rubbed her finger over her chin and shook it in the air as she laughed. "Burt! I knew you would come back. Did you change jobs? Are you working for ONE R&D now?"

"Something like that," he replied. "And it's good to hear your voice. What are we doing today? I am simply here to watch, notate, and be of service if you need me to."

Stephanie nodded, extended her hands, and felt the energy bounce off her palms. "I think I will simply go with it today. I have a thought, but I want to work with Meligornian magic first. So, I'll only be doing some manipulations."

"All right," BURT replied. "Whenever you are ready. Just pretend I'm not here."

She glanced around and smirked before she closed her eyes. Her focus immediate, she used her hands to draw the energy slowly from the ground and twirl it in circular motions in front of her. As the energy grew stronger, she moved her arms faster and whipped the long trails of magic through the air so they twisted and twined together before they unraveled and began again. She tilted her head back and opened her mouth. The magic flowed from her throat and seeped from the corners of her closed eyes.

Eventually, the stream of energy coming in began to slow and she glowed brighter and brighter. The streams she still connected to spiraled around and through her, back out again, and passed through each fingertip. She dipped her head low and continued to sway as if in a tribal dance as she looped her arms down and then high over her head. The circle of magic grew tighter and she twirled it in her hands as if she were a goddess playing with the very solar system itself.

When she opened her eyes, the magic within her erupted to join the intertwining strands around her. Purple vibrations coursed down each strand of her hair and the flowers began to shimmer and change shape before they fell to the ground.

BURT paused for a moment when he identified a sound from the space. The deep humming seemed to be a song from the pit of Stephanie's stomach. Each note hung on the strings of energy that swirled through her at an ever-increasing pace. Her entire body glowed so brightly, the system was filled with a momentary white noise. Suddenly, she froze, her feet raised from the ground, and her breath caught in her throat.

For a moment, everything was absolutely silent until…*booom!* Her entire body exploded and launched waves of energy to blast outward and destroy the building she stood in. It flattened the long blades of grass and shoved the simulated MU spectrum in the sky aside.

It took BURT a split second to gather his system back to a baseline but as soon as he did, he ejected her body from the system. The door to the pod flew open and Stephanie rolled out and fell on all fours. She rasped a ragged cough and the spit dribbled from her mouth onto the cushioned pads. When she opened her eyes, everything was so bright—so real. She blinked wildly and stared in bemusement at the string of saliva attached to her lip. When she wiped her mouth with the back of her hand, she noticed blood. Reluctantly, she looked at the spittle on the floor and saw telltale streaks of red in that as well.

She had done it again, despite her knowledge of the first time. She had done something to her real body through her virtual world experience.

CHAPTER TEN

Stephanie wiped her face with a towel and took another big swig of water. She felt better—much better—but she still couldn't understand what had happened. Ms. E had come in and helped her up off the floor, brought the doc in to check her out, and everything seemed fine. As soon as she got some water in her system and the batteries back in her pocket, she felt as right as rain, physically at least. It was a little confusing that the battery somehow seemed to make her stronger—unless she subconsciously absorbed a little of it in her weakened state? The thought was worth exploring but at another time. Right now, she was content to simply accept its help because she had much larger issues to confront.

What she had seen within the energy she had experienced while in the pod was something she couldn't even begin to explain.

Ms. E walked in and clapped her hands. She wore her normal clothes, including the six-inch heels. For the life of her, Stephanie couldn't figure out how she actually walked in the things. "How are you feeling, kiddo?"

She nodded. "Good. Am I going back in?"

The woman smiled mischievously. "Not exactly. Okay, come on in, boys."

Stephanie sat and watched as six guys, all relatively young, all buff, and all dressed the exact same way in ONE R&D workout gear, walked into the room. Ms. E stood to the side and cracked her knuckles. "So, with the way the world is today, together with the way that some people may view you as an asset or a liability—both with equally detrimental side effects, I should add—we think it is vitally important that you know some self-defense."

She wrinkled her nose in distaste at a flash of memory. "I learned some martial arts at Pinnacle when I hooked the cubes up at night."

Ms. E chuckled. "That's good. It means you have a base in all of this, but you need to know it real-world style. Most likely, if you are fighting for your life, it will be in the real world. This is also an excellent time for you to really get to know your security crew for the building. They will be your first, middle, and last line of defense."

She put her arm out and moved down the line. "These are your six primary guards. There are four others who give these guys a break from time to time. We have Brenden, Avery, Johnny, Jack—or Frog, as we call him—Marcus, and you have already met Lars."

Lars gave her a small flick of the fingers and a smile. She nodded at them but slyly edged her hand into the pocket of her pants to grasp the battery. This seemed like as good a time as any to practice with the energy. The batteries the company had sent her had enabled her to practice, and in time, she'd found that she could absorb and hold a small residual level of the power. Nothing even close to a major breakthrough, but encouraging, nonetheless. She'd simply assumed that her body had adjusted somewhat.

This was a small battery and wasn't completely full, either, so it was a good basis for experimentation. She kept her expression relaxed as she drew all the remaining energy from the battery as slowly as she could so that Ms. E wouldn't notice. A little tour earlier had revealed that she could reload them inside the building. It seemed the company had invested in a supply of the larger ones as a kind of magical larder, and she assumed they would be replaced as they were used. Knowing that, she didn't mind depleting this one in what might be a good cause.

She took a deep breath. "I'm fighting my own guys?"

Ms. E nodded. "I thought that would be a better way to start than to fight your enemies."

Stephanie stood and stretched her arms from side to side. "Let me clarify this because it can be a gray area in my world. Am I using all my abilities?"

The woman smirked and turned to the men. "For the first few rounds, I want Stephanie to restrain herself. We will work on martial arts."

They exchanged glances and finally looked at Stephanie, who seemed really small compared to everyone else. Having never actually seen her do anything outside the videos of her that they'd watched, they simply shrugged. Ms. E stepped out of the way and stood on the side where she leaned her shoulder against one of the columns.

Stephanie walked into the center and adopted her defensive pose. Her self-confidence rose when all the knowledge and muscle memory from school suddenly flooded her head. Brenden came forward first with the task to ensure that she knew all the defensive moves. She blocked him with the simpler ones, but when he did a back handspring and brought his foot around, he knocked her squarely in the head.

Immediately, his eyes widened, and he went to grab her. Ms. E shook her head. "She has to be able to handle this on her own. Now she knows there is more than only her nose and mouth to defend."

As she stood and snatched the mouth guard made for her off

the table, Stephanie's lip twitched with irritation. She slipped it in and jumped back and forth as she rolled her shoulders. Next was Avery to teach her upper body offensive moves. She flowed through the attack movements the cube had taught her and tried to keep her feet from leaving the mat as she moved. She was supposed to only work her upper body in this exercise. He blocked her at every pass but one in which he shifted, grabbed her arm, and twisted it behind her back.

He released her when she grunted her surrender. She moved on to Johnny, who worked hard with her on lower body movements. Every time she flailed a limb, he would smack it down. "Control. You have to control every movement you make. Every movement is deliberate. It is made for you to push through. It is for you to control. Then, and only then, can you adjust the speed and placement at a moment's notice."

She gritted her teeth and kicked harder, swirled around, and pounded her leg into his arm, leg, and chest. When she thought she would almost die of exhaustion, Jack jumped in and she suddenly realized why they called him Frog. He bounced continually and his feet moved rapidly as his legs pistoned in constant attack. She had to put it all together and use her arms, her upper torso, her bottom, her legs—everything—in a fluid, seamless motion to fight back.

Although he was faster than her, a couple of knockdowns soon pushed her into the zone. Her eyes and senses became hyper-focused on every twitch of his body and every tense and release of his muscles. She found herself able to anticipate some of his movements, something she had never been able to focus enough to do. It wasn't like she spent her childhood sparring every day.

She vaulted into the air, kicked, and barely missed his head. He flipped under and she landed, her thigh on his shoulder and knee bent over the front of him. With a laugh, he bounced and flung her over and onto her back. She grunted as she rolled across the floor, thankful there were at least mats down at that point.

Ms. E waved her hand to Lars and Marcus. "You two start out two on one. Stephanie, when you think you have the balls for another, you tap the mat. Each time you single tap, we send in another. When I call full action, it's you against the six of them."

Stephanie rubbed her nose and cracked her neck before she gave the thumbs-up. She smacked her hands together and leaned down to study her two opponents. Without warning, she raced forward and used her feet to push off the mat and launch herself at the men. She struck Lars's thigh and twisted, ran the back of her foot over the side of his face, and continued across Marcus' as well.

She landed in a squatted position with one hand on the mat, her head up and ready for retribution. Both men laughed as they shook the daze from their heads. She tapped the mat, tapped it again, and held up two fingers.

Lars clapped his hands in approval. "That's right. Never give up. Always ask for more."

The group cheered as Frog and Johnny strutted out. It was now four to one, and she felt good. Even if she knew she would probably get her ass kicked.

They came at her one at a time at first. Johnny was blocked but Frog slammed her down hard on the mat. She bounced up and hurtled forward to attack Lars. Marcus slipped in and ducked low at the last second to take her out at the knees. She flipped over him, grasped Lars as she spun, and hauled him down with her. The guys watching jumped up, yelled, and held the sides of their heads in a gesture of exasperation.

Ms. E smiled. "Five seconds to full action!"

Stephanie chuckled and smirked at Lars as she pulled her mouth guard out and spat blood into a bucket on the sidelines. All six men gathered in the arena. Stephanie made her way into the middle as Ms. E counted down to the last second. When she blew the whistle, Stephanie could tell she wouldn't be able to take them down without a little help. At first, she simply energized herself a little to give her extra speed to grab one of her opponents before they could react.

She gripped Johnny's wrist and turned to bring his arm over her shoulder backward. She grunted as she bounced on her feet, but she couldn't for the life of her flip him over her back. Cautiously, she held her breath and released a little more magic to give her the ability to fling him up and over her. She managed to give herself possibly a little too much since he careened off the mat and into the wall. Everyone looked at him and he put his hand up. "Fine. I'm fine. Keep going."

At that point, she was tired of restraint. As Frog bounced toward her, she swayed and swished her arms to the side in his direction. A gust of wind struck him in mid-leap, rammed into his stomach, and flipped him head over heels. He landed on his ass, his legs out straight, and bounced a couple of feet before he groaned and toppled to clutch his family jewels. Stephanie grinned. She used to think the expression outdated and old-fashioned, but he hung onto them like they were both family and fortune, so maybe it was still appropriate after all.

Marcus lunged at her, but she was too quick for him and rolled to the right. She stamped her foot hard on the floor and shook the ground beneath him. He put his arms out in an effort to keep his balance and she snickered, grabbed one, and spun faster and faster. She aimed downward and let go and he slid helplessly across to the other side of the room. Instantly, both Avery and Brenden were on her. She kicked and punched, dodged their shots, and only managed a couple of strong punches once or twice. Not enough to knock them down, though, and it soon became clear that she needed to up her game.

She backed up several feet, raised her arms high, and fisted her hands. She dropped and smacked them down on the ground. Flames erupted in front of them, as tall as the men were. They couldn't have hurt them since they were simply Meligornian magic tricks, but it distracted them long enough for her to vault over them, land, and grasp Avery around the neck. She used her momentum to flip him and drive his body into the floor.

Brenden saw it and tried to go in while still fanning the flames away. She smiled and pushed off with her shoulders, launched upward, and kicked him hard under the chin. He teetered for a moment but went down hard. Slowly, she stood, breathing heavily, and wiped the sweat from her hands. She stared at the flames for a minute and wondered if Lars had simply chickened out or if he waited for the right moment.

Stephanie chuckled and moved toward the flames. "You know they aren't real, right? You don't have to be afraid of some big, bad blue flames, Lars."

As her gaze refocused, her face dropped. Lars rocketed through the flames, his fists clenched and muscles tight, and he growled and yelled loudly. As his arm came for her neck, she cringed. "Oh, my…this is gonna hurt."

He bulldozed into her, twisted his body around her, and secured her in a choke hold. She gripped his huge arm and spluttered as her face turned red. As the blood drained from her brain, she slapped his arm ineffectually. They both dropped to their knees and he laughed. "It's okay. Just go to sleep, then. Lars will take care of the rough stuff."

Her eyes flew open and blue flickered in her irises. While she knew she didn't have much left, she wouldn't let him get the best of her. She mustered the last reserve of magic she had and drew it into her fingertip.

Lars snickered and pulled it tighter. "Surrender. Double-tap my arm and you will breathe again, ma'am. Just give in. It's okay not to be the best yet. Say it—I surrender."

She choked out a couple of words and the man leaned closer. "What was that?"

He released a smidgeon of pressure and she yelled her defiance, her voice raspy. *"Like hell I will, shode!"*

She twisted her arm and jammed her finger into his side to release a blast of electricity. He immediately locked up and spit dribbled down his lip. She ducked out of his hold and turned toward him, breathing heavily, and leaned forward to his ear with a giggle. "Didn't you teach me to never surrender only a few minutes ago?"

Unable to resist the temptation, she poked him again. A small spark toppled him easily and he jerked spasmodically on the mat. She stood, raised her hands, and managed a short laugh before she stumbled backward and dropped from exhaustion. Ms. E laughed and ran over to scoop Stephanie up in her arms.

Frog shambled to his feet and still rubbed himself a little awkwardly. "Take care of these idiots," the woman said and gestured to the wounded with her head.

She turned and carried Stephanie out of the room. "C'mon to the medical doc, little miss spent battery."

The crew remained on the floor of the workout room and they groaned as the four backup guards and Frog finally helped them up and dragged them to the bench. The four replacements had cheered Stephanie on from the sidelines the whole time, thankful that it wasn't their turn yet.

CHAPTER ELEVEN

Lars stood in front of Stephanie, his hands out in front of him in a gesture that seemed both placating and a protest at the same time. The others lingered in the background, some bruised and others fighting through the pain. "We understand that your martial arts abilities are, without magic, on par with ours. But what we cannot compete with is when you use your magic together with them."

She bit her bottom lip and looked at him with raised eyebrows. "So, what are you saying? Do you want me to go easy on you guys?"

The other men attempted to stand, puff their chests out, and shake their heads, and she smirked as Lars waved his hands at them and rubbed his chin.

"No, but we want to learn more about them and understand your power so that we can then understand how we are supposed to help protect you. That is our job, after all. And if someone does come for you, they are either stupid or they are strong as well. If we faced six of you out there, we wouldn't stand a chance."

Stephanie nodded and rolled her shoulder to ease the pain.

"Well, as of right now, I'm the only one anyone knows of. But I get what you're saying and honestly, if I have you guys to back me up or protect me, I want you to know how it all works. The problem with that is that I don't really know how it all works yet. That is part of why I'm here. To figure that out."

Lars's mouth hung open for a moment and he tapped his fingers distractedly against his legs. "Right. I get it. Well, I guess all we can do is keep practicing against you and do what we can to learn. When you've figured it all out, we can go from there."

The team in the background groaned. She chuckled and peered over Lars's shoulder. "It's okay, guys. I won't kick your asses so hard next time."

Frog cheered and the others gave him a nasty look. He lowered his arm slowly and glanced away, trying not to make any eye contact at all. Elizabeth walked up and patted Lars on the shoulder. "Get your men cleaned up. I'll put the other four on temp watch until you can walk straight. And for crying out loud, get Frog a cup, please. Actually, all of you get some cups."

The man nodded at them both and hurried off. Elizabeth put her arm around the girl's shoulders and smiled as they walked away. "I think you hurt not only their manhood but their sensibility as well."

Stephanie giggled. "I didn't mean to. I simply went with an attack. Right now, I want to study my transfer of energy more. What happened in the pod was kinda freaky and I would like that not to happen on Earth to my real body."

Elizabeth sighed. "Yeah, us too. Listen, we have a room for you here. It's not the hotel, but it's definitely put together. I did it myself—with the guys lugging all the heavy shit, of course. We took the liberty to grab your stuff from the hotel and put it all in your room. Is that okay? I thought you might be safer here for now. It's almost a compound of sorts."

"That's fine. It will keep me closer to the whole pod thing and means less time in flying cars."

Elizabeth laughed as she showed her to her room. "We'll do a lesson or two in the pod. It shouldn't take you too long to catch on to that one."

Stephanie stopped as a slight sense of unease settled over her. She realized that she'd allowed her excitement over the new job, the opportunity to study and explore through the pod, and the rush of being important enough to dine with ambassadors and have her own protective detail go to her head. Not once had she questioned anything, aside from her responses in and to the pod and the magic. Everything else had been shoved aside, but a dozen questions now crowded in to unsettle her.

"What's wrong?" Ms. E asked and placed her hand on Stephanie's arm.

"I...not wrong, exactly, but... I have so many questions suddenly. Like why we moved from the old building instead of rebuilding after the fire. And why you've brought me to live in a...what did you call it? A compound, with a whole security detail twenty-four-seven. Did something happen? Am I in danger?"

The other woman sighed but her expression seemed more weary than upset. "I know you have questions, kiddo, and they will all be answered—in time. What I can tell you is that you have a rare talent—a gift—and there are many people out there who would like to gain control of that, whether it benefits you or not. We'd like to be sure that you're prepared for it should anyone discover you and try to take advantage of you."

Stephanie nodded as a quick vision of Pinnacle surfaced. She already knew first-hand that very few people would really care what happened to her along the way. All they would want was to feed their greed and power—with her as the main course.

"I guess..." She shrugged. "There's so much I still don't understand—like how the energy really works and what it can do and how. And the martial arts, too. Seriously? I didn't think of it at the time, but how is it possible that I could hold my own against six grown men when the only training I had—if you can actually call it training—was a night plugged into a cube? None of it makes any sense at all."

Ms. E smiled. "No, it doesn't. But it's real, Steph. The truth is that we don't have the answers either. The best we can do is to create a safe environment in which you can learn—and that includes teaching you how to defend yourself using all your abilities. Honestly, we're learning as we go, like you are. But at least with us, you have a say in what happens. You can trust us to not force you beyond what you're comfortable with. We see the potential in you to make a difference, and we want you to reach your full potential—for your own sake as much as for all those people out there whose lives you could impact down the line." She smiled and squeezed her hand. "Do you trust us?"

Despite the sudden rush of questions and the sense of disquiet that still hovered, Stephanie looked at her companion and nodded. Instinct, if not common sense, told her that the people who had stepped up and who now surrounded her were possibly the only ones she could trust.

Ms. E opened the door and let Stephanie in, smiled again as she closed it, and left her to herself. The whole room was painted in purple and black, the colors she couldn't seem to get away from. She didn't mind, though. It looked nice and felt familiar. She picked a tablet up from a small round table by the door and started to press buttons randomly. What she thought were solid painted walls were actually holographic and shifted to various scenes from all over the galaxy. From floating in deep space to laying in a field on Meligorn, she could choose to be anywhere.

Stephanie stopped on a nighttime scene from Meligorn and stared at the Towers and the planets in the distance. She put the tablet down and walked to the closet, opened it, and grinned at all her clothes hung neatly in a row. Her suitcases were stored in the bottom and the rest of her belongings were placed either on the carved wooden dresser with vines etched on all sides, in the bathroom—also holographic and similar to the one in the hotel—or in her drawers.

She wandered back into the room and froze as a sudden fear knifed through her—the book. With a sharp surge of panic, she whirled toward her king-sized four-poster bed and puffed out a relieved breath. She had tried to secure it with magic but honestly hadn't been all that reassured. The energy might have protected it from harm, but there was no way to know if it would have kept it safe from curious fingers. The thought that it might have been stolen—although why would anyone want it, anyway?—left her with a real sense of loss.

A long sigh of relief started her breathing again. The book rested there on the end of the bed, wrapped in the purple velvet. She sat slowly beside it and rubbed her hand over the fabric. While she knew there were things combat-related she needed to take care of, she didn't want to focus as much on the military side of the esoteric.

One thing that she had learned—and she had kept this to herself up to that point—was that Earth already had the energy that she needed. The problem was, humanity had lost the abilities and genetics, for the most part, to handle it. Therefore, in their minds, it simply didn't exist. Her focus now would need to be to learn more of that.

But in that moment, there was nothing more she could really do. She did find it nice that she had a place that was at least semi-permanent to lay her head at night. As much as she liked the hotel, it was still simply that—a hotel. The only two people she would really miss were Rufus and her AI, Sarah. Stephanie stuck her bottom lip out when she thought about her companion Sarah. She was only a computer, but nonetheless, she was a good listener.

"Well, I guess I'll have to go it alone. Thanks for all your companionship, Sarah," she said out loud and pulled her book into her lap.

"You're welcome," Sarah replied. "Although I don't think you will have to go it alone. I was brought over in the system to stay with you. My laugh was permanently disabled."

Stephanie giggled and suddenly felt a whole lot more cheerful. "That is great news. It definitely feels better like that."

The AI paused. "Enjoy your reading and let me know when you are ready for dinner. I believe the kitchen is down the hall."

She nodded. "Will do."

Carefully, she unwound the fabric from the book, opened it, and placed her fingers on the paper. She had enough energy in her to draw the words into her mind. It was a journal from an ancestor many centuries in the past.

This diary will give the reader an understanding of what I believe happened to the family from the first Morgana, from whom we trace our lineage.

Stephanie settled in, pulled her legs up, and crossed them. She continued reading. **As she was a child born out of wedlock, we find lineage to another child born of her. This child was also born out of wedlock and not inscribed in the annals of time except to our own books. We are the ones who bear witness to protect the Earth as Morgana might have, had her family not betrayed her first.**

Her eyes opened and she sat motionless for several moments, thinking about those words. Morgana was a first name, apparently, not a last name, or had been so at the beginning. She still didn't have enough information on who Morgana was, so she put the book down carefully on the bed and retrieved her personal tablet from the desk. Once she'd placed it in the center of the bed, she pressed the button to bring the screen into interactive mode. The image popped up from the display like a hologram.

"Tell me more about Morgana," she said.

The avatar on the screen pretended to wander around and search for information until it finally stuck one finger in the air and yelled, "Eureka!" It tossed a bunch of papers into the air that became the pages for her to scroll through. One by one, she swiped to each one and read bits and pieces of information from folklore and legend. After a few of these, she came to a darker site—one that required her thumbprint to enter. Assuming it wouldn't work since she had never been to it, she hovered her thumb over the reader. The print flittered on the screen and then turned gold and the site opened immediately. Stephanie stared at it for a moment, astonished that it had worked, but decided not to question the thumbprint issue too deeply. Information was more important at this point.

She read through the trials and the tribulations of the Morgana children and the hatred and anger toward them. They were bastards, born out of wedlock, their fathers usually far away and their lives torturous. Stephanie, although she had never met her father, had never been treated poorly. Mark had been in her life since she was old enough to remember and her parents loved her with everything in them. But she still bore the name and the powers that seemed to go along with it.

Soon after, she came to a picture of a woman. She was dressed in a black calf-length dress with a white collar, a white jacket that looked almost like a man's sports coat, white slim-looking lace-up leather shoes, stockings, and a wide-brimmed hat. Her hair cascaded in large wavy curls, pinned back behind her ears. She had a beautiful smile, and her eyes looked amazingly familiar.

Stephanie continued to read. "Maddalena Morgana, born in 1919, no father on record. In history books, for humans without the gift, Maddalena was known to have helped the Allies in WWII by creating a spycraft that assisted in infiltrating the enemy. To this day, the non-gifted cannot explain the spycraft, nor did they ever retrieve it from enemy lines. The truth was, Maddalena was the next gifted Morgana to be born on this earth. Her powers were strong in precognition. It wasn't a spycraft that aided the allies, but instead, it was her dreams of the future which helped the Allies, especially on D-Day. Maddalena was more gifted than anyone in that time would have ever understood, and after WWII ended, she disappeared from the public eye, never to be seen again."

Stephanie swiped the screen away, chewed on her lip, and twirled her finger around the end of her ponytail. So, Morgana had gone from being the first name of the original one to the last name. It made sense. She was born illegitimately, and her mother's maiden name was Morgana, which Stephanie still kept legally, so she could be considered the next Morgana in line.

Her thoughts now rampant, she stood, set the tablet aside, and began to pace the room. A number of things began to crystallize within her. She loved her last name but because of the sound of it, not because of a previously child-like need to be different. She had always felt a strange attachment to it. It would only make sense, then, that her mother had pushed her to take Mark's last name to hide the Morgana last name. Mark had been in her life since she was a baby but had not married her mother for many years due to adoption policies and issues with marriage qualifications during a particularly troubling time in Federation history.

By the time he did, she was given the choice, and she kept Morgana without a thought. All those times that her mother had begged her, snapped at her, and fought with her over the name was not for Mark's sake, it was for hers. It was not to hurt her stepdad's feelings. He always understood. It had been for her mother because she knew the history—or at least tales of it—and it frightened her, as it would any mother. So she tried to shadow it out, put the past in the past, change the name, and move on from it, but it wasn't something that Stephanie could run from. It was who she was, last name or not.

Then again, there was a part of her mother that, no matter how much she might fear something, she pushed herself to not believe it. It was like not believing in the superstition of the number thirteen but then building a hotel and leaving floor thirteen out of the plans. When Stephanie started fooling with magic and revealed that she had the gift, her mother hadn't actually seemed all that shocked. If she were anyone else, her mother would have lost it, but she was calm and even seemed to know what to do in the first circumstance when she saved that woman's life.

Stephanie walked to the wall and stood there to stare out into the virtual space. Part of her wished she could leap out, float to Meligorn, and find more answers. At the same time, the Earth had all the answers that she would need. She merely had to figure them out without completely blowing herself up in the process. Before that day, she would have thought of that as an easy request, but it wasn't in the least. In fact, it was more of a warning now that she had done it in the Virtual World without even thinking. Things constantly became more and more complicated as the days passed but brought very few answers in the meantime. Answers were exactly what she needed, and time seemed determined to make the power inside her stronger and stronger. It would only be a matter of time before she or someone she loved got hurt.

CHAPTER TWELVE

The next day came all too quickly, and Stephanie hadn't slept much at all. It was a good thing then, that both BURT and Elizabeth had decided that she should have some lessons on how to act around other people. It wasn't only how to act around dignitaries, species from other planets, or people she revealed her magic to, but people in general.

She was no longer the young Stephanie Morgana who kept as low a profile as possible and everyone looked right past her. She had already been hounded by so many different people, from the media to companies that wanted her to be a part of something they had going on. As she progressed and her reputation grew, as it inevitably would, she would come under increasing pressure. As tempting as it might be, she couldn't simply shock every single person who tried to talk her into leaving ONE R&D. She had to learn how to handle herself in high society as well as on the street.

The class only lasted for about six earth hours, three in the pod. When she came out, Elizabeth held her robe out for her with a smile on her face. "I'm glad to see you didn't fall out of the pod this time."

Stephanie put her arms in the robe and wrapped it around herself before she turned to face her. "Thank you for helping me. I don't remember it but thank you."

The woman tapped her on the shoulder. "That's my job, sister. I can't have you stroking out on the first day. It would look bad on my resume."

She laughed as they wandered to the door, exited, and locked the pod room behind them. Lars and Frog stood guard outside the room and both glanced away when she emerged in her robe. She chuckled and put her hand up to give Lars a high-five.

When she reached her room, Elizabeth glanced toward the kitchen. "I'll make lunch soon. Why don't you call and check in with your family and friends and center yourself a little today? If you're hungry, food will be there. I'll have Sarah tell you when it's done."

Stephanie nodded, entered her room, and closed the door behind her. She walked to the bed and lay down before she set her tablet up in front of her. Once she'd checked that her robe was tied tightly, she called her parents. Her mom's face came up on the screen and she smiled warmly. "Hi, honey!"

A warmth flooded her chest and flushed on her cheeks. "Hi, Mom. Hi, Dad!"

Her dad stuck his head into the camera view. "Hey, kiddo. Love you!"

"Love you." She giggled.

Her mom smiled. "We are right in the middle of training additional staff for the new client's building. I have to admit that to get it exactly how they want it, with as many floors as there are, is extremely challenging, and we have definitely had to bring additional people on. But we are so excited to work with them. I spoke to Mr. Martelle and he couldn't say enough good things about you."

Stephanie laughed. "Yeah, he got to see a whole bunch of

different sides of me that day. The assertive, the business, and the magical. I let him see it all, good and bad. I guess it worked."

"Because you're adorable and you know how to talk to people." Her mom grinned. "So, how is everything there? Are you in a new room?"

She looked around. "Oh, yeah. I moved from the hotel into the compound. They have a really nice private room for me, my own pod that I can use anytime I like, and security staff as well. It's easiest if I stay here and I actually like it. This is somewhere I can feel comfortable instead of that constant hotel feeling, no matter how nice it is. Oh, and they brought the AI from my hotel room over because I liked her so much."

Her mother laughed. "That's what I'm talking about. Take care of my baby girl. I want you to be happy and safe, that's all."

Stephanie nodded. "And I am both of those things. But Mom, I actually hoped I could talk to you about something. It has to do with the book you gave me."

After a short silence, her mother cleared her throat and stepped away from whoever she was close to. "You want to talk about your name."

"Yeah."

Cindy's gaze shifted back and forth and the forced smile on her lips twitched. "There are things which we discuss in person only. I cannot read the diary, but I realize you can. When we see each other, I will chat to you about it."

She knew she wouldn't say any more and that she had been as clear as she could be in that moment. This was a huge deal—a huge secret—and they couldn't risk a discussion about it over the phone or video in case someone had tapped the lines or transmitted the video somewhere else. Although disappointed, Stephanie simply nodded, gave her mom a wink, and changed the subject.

"I forgot, I haven't talked to you in a couple of days," she said excitedly. "I had a real glass of champagne the other day. Well, a quarter of a glass because I had to leave, but champagne nonetheless."

Her mother's eyes glistened. "Oh, champagne. We miss that bubbly wonderfulness. I've always wanted to pop a bottle and celebrate...well, anything really. That's wonderful, darling. I hope that one day, your father and I will have the chance to do such exciting things."

Stephanie's eyes went soft and she breathed out a heavy breath. "You will. I'll make sure you have the chance to. What is life for if you don't get to experience all of it, right? Not only the struggles, that's not fair."

Cindy nodded, pressed her lips together, and cleared her throat. Her eyes glistened as she nodded at Stephanie's father off-screen. "Sweetie, oh, I miss talking to you so much, but unfortunately, until we get this building business taken care of, we are pushing against the clock. When I'm not there, I'm hiring people, putting them through training, getting our equipment cleaned, the whole nine yards. We're using some of our daytime sites to train extra staff as well to speed things up a little, which is why there are others here with us. It's a crazy train here at home."

"I'll let you go then. I can call you some other time in the evening," Stephanie offered. "I just finished my morning session and didn't even think of the time. Although with a night shift as well now, I'm not sure how you and Dad have scheduled your off time."

Her mother waved her hands. "Nor should you ever worry about that. Never hesitate to call me when you have a few minutes to do it. I would rather talk while cleaning than miss you altogether because you have such a busy schedule too. Once we have the logistics ironed out, things will be better all round."

"I want to come back home very soon so I can see you guys. Or maybe, when you get a break, bring you out here to DC so you can see all the historical sites and all the flying cars and craziness over here. Chicago will be like that eventually."

Her mother shook her head. "That would be lovely. And sweetheart, I want you to know how much I love you. You were meant to be special, you just didn't know it."

Stephanie waved goodbye to her father and they ended the call. Her mother, no matter how scared or worried she was, always had the ability to make her feel better. She always knew the right thing to say in any situation. Comfortably cross-legged on the bed, she thought about home and all her nice walks to school and home each day. How simple her life had been only a year before when taking the Federation Exams was nothing more than a blip in her future. Things got so crazy so fast, but that was okay because she would slowly figure out who she was.

Thinking about home, she looked at her watch and remembered that Wednesdays were when Todd had his mid-morning free period. She had completely forgotten about that and, excited to hear his voice, she swiped her tablet and called him. He answered on the second ring and appeared in front of himself in hologram form to salute her.

Stephanie laughed and saluted him awkwardly in response. "I didn't join the Federation. Why would you salute me?"

Todd rolled his eyes with a smirk on his face. "Because it's not all about you, butthead."

She looked at him, suddenly serious. "Did you? Already? You're not even out of school yet."

He shook his head. "No, but I have found myself a certified navy recruiter. I barely even spoke to anyone before and she kind of found me. I guess through the Federation testing results or something. Anyway..." Todd wiggled his eyebrows. "She's a female, cause I. Am. Hot."

Stephanie raised an eyebrow. "I'm not busting your model bubble or anything but remember the recruiters for the class before us. They basically sent either the doppelganger of the person they tried to recruit or the hot girl or guy for those less...intellectual."

"Are you calling me a dud?" He narrowed his eyes.

Stephanie giggled and snorted. "No. But that's great, dude. If that is what *you* want, not what the pretty girl is telling you to do. Signing up for the Federation is way longer term than going on some weird kale and celery diet for a few weeks."

Todd scoffed and gestured dismissively. "I got this. I've always known I would go in but I'm waiting to see where they put me. Hopefully, something cool and not merely a long drive out into the darkness to meet my maker. Oh, and there was a guy looking for you, but I told him you were gone, and that I had interest. Wham, bam, thank you, ma'am, I was looked up by a Petty Officer First Class 'Wowzah' Santino. She called these digits only one week later. Tanned skin, curvy, uniform fits just right. Red lipstick, smells like flowers, laughs at my jokes, and basically can't live without me at this point."

She shook her head. "The Toddster has fallen in love."

In response, he rolled his eyes and pulled on the neckline of his T-shirt. "The ladies have fallen in love with the Toddster. It was bound to happen. They saw you disappear out of the picture and figured they could slide right in and not have to worry about you setting them on magical fire."

Stephanie pursed her lips. "Nope, they still need to worry about that one. So, when will you start everything?"

Todd shrugged and sighed. "I'll have my first tests done this weekend. I really hope I do well on them."

She gave him a reassuring look as if she were touching his shoulder through the video. "Dude, I know you will. I'm really happy for you. I know this is actually what you wanted."

He continued to talk, and Stephanie's thoughts drifted off for a moment. Would it be naïve to think that they might have done all of that for her?

Stephanie shook her head and pulled her attention back to Todd. *Or, Stephanie Morgana, am I now starting to believe everything is about me?*

CHAPTER THIRTEEN

When Stephanie finally got off the phone with Todd, she felt better about being in her new position and her new life. She had a shit ton of questions that needed to be answered, but there was no elucidation that could be given to her at that time. The facts eluded her at every turn, but what did she really expect? She was a descendant or manifestation of what could potentially be a magical human from centuries before. Fair enough, she hadn't actually found anything that would confirm the magical part of the equation, but given her experience, it seemed very likely. The only ancestor whom she could find any real information on was basically a war hero who had helped the Allies win the war. After that, she disappeared.

Disappearing didn't seem all that crazy, though, especially when people close to the government and people in her social circle knew about her abilities. From the little time Stephanie had spent in the spotlight, she could feel that pressure mounting. And from the way that Elizabeth, Burt, and the others attempted to protect her, she knew that harder times most likely lay ahead. Still, she would persist because the information she discovered had the ability to change everything. There was no doubt that for anyone below the middle-class line, and many above it, change was in the wind.

Stephanie put her tablet on the dresser and pulled the drawers out to skim through her clothes. She grabbed a pair of ripped jeans, an old vintage Chicago Cubs T-shirt Todd had given her one year for her birthday, and a baseball cap. She needed to get out of there, to clear her mind and do something that didn't involve magic, or research, or questioning every damn thing in her life. She simply wanted to be a normal old human for a while.

Knowing how crazy they were about keeping her safe, though, Stephanie headed to the kitchen in the hope that Ms. E was still there. As she turned the corner, Elizabeth glanced up, her outfit beyond incongruous. She wore a chef's apron with her business attire and six-inch heels. It didn't really fit, but she seemed to be in a good mood, nonetheless.

She glanced at the girl's outfit and looked at the cutting board as she chopped celery. "Are you thinking of going out?"

Stephanie leaned against the doorway and shoved her hands in her pockets. "Yeah. I really wanted some me time, I guess, but I thought I should check with you."

A smile pulled at the woman's lips. "Remember, I am your boss on the clock, not your mom. But, now that you mention it, yes. I don't mind you going out as long as you take a couple of the guys with you."

She nodded. "K. I'll swing in and see who has the aches and who is reasonably functional. I'm sure you'll know when I'm back."

Elizabeth chuckled. "I know most things, and if I miss something, the system will have logged it anyway."

Stephanie smirked as she headed off to the guard's living quarters. She poked her head into the common area where Lars sat at the table and Frog sprawled on the couch. "Where is everyone?'

Lars glanced up and smiled. "On duty. It's me and Frog's time off. Two of the subs took care of our shifts."

She pursed her lips and rocked back and forth on her feet. "Okay. Well, maybe you can point me in the right direction, then. I want to go into town and spend some 'me' time out there. Elizabeth wants me to take two guys with me. Who should I ask?"

Frog glanced at the other man and shrugged. Lars looked at the notes he was taking and shut the book. "Give us ten and we'll head out with you."

Stephanie grinned. "Thanks. I'll go get a car to pull around."

The guys changed and traveled with Stephanie as she clung to the "oh shit" handle in the flying car. It docked three stories up and let them out into a docking terminal that led down into the city. It was the old Dupont Circle where statues that had been erected a short time before the 2094 riots for social justice and equality now crumbled in the center. That was one of the main events in their history that were studied because, like so many other social justice causes, nothing really ever changed. Maybe the wording of a law or two, but nothing significant.

The streets were busy with tourists and business persons on their late lunches or errands. Although you could tell there had been historical periods of unrest in the area, the commemorated ideals of keeping the place as accurate as possible to the original architecture seemed to be upheld. It was pleasant, like walking through an old town filled with commerce and political accents.

Stephanie wandered somewhat aimlessly, stopped for a pretzel, and window-shopped most of the time. Lars and Frog followed without complaint. They gave her enough space to feel alone but still kept a watchful eye out. Stephanie meandered down the streets and gazed at the buildings and the flying cars zooming overhead.

"Uh, Steph," Lars said a short while later and jogged up beside her.

She shook the daze from her head. "Yeah?"

His gaze traced up the street. "Maybe we should head back toward the circle. We've wandered too far and there are a lot of places around here that can be dangerous and secluded."

Stephanie focused on her surroundings and realized that he was right. She had wandered off the beaten path to an area of town that mostly consisted of crumbling buildings, graffiti, and random places where scantily clad women stood on porches. The duo exchanged a nod and turned quickly but stopped in their tracks. Frog froze, put a hand around to his back, and gripped the laser pistol shoved into the waistband of his pants.

Up ahead, four men with orange bandanas tied around their arms and sparkling gold teeth strolled toward them. The one in the front sucked on his front tooth with his tongue and an eerie smirk pulled at his lips. "Well, lookie here, guys. If it isn't our lucky day. We have the Earth Witch right in front of us."

One of the men behind him smiled, a twinkle in his eye. He flipped his toothpick from one side of his mouth to the other and a hand slid into his jacket. "I heard there's a nice reward for bringing her in. A lot of high profiles are looking to dig into that pretty little head of hers."

Frog moved his gun around slowly and backed up beside Stephanie and Lars. "I would suggest you guys keep moving. The only place she is going is back home."

The mustached man laughed and whistled. Lars, Stephanie, and Frog moved closer together as six more thugs appeared from the dark recesses of the alleys. The leader twisted his lips from a smile to a snarl. "It looks like you'll have to make us."

The guy to the side of the gang leader drew faster than Frog could. A hail of bullets struck the guard and catapulted him back. Immediately, Lars grabbed Stephanie and shoved her in one direction as he dove in the other and blasted his weapon at the group. A barrage erupted as guns fired from all angles. Stephanie pressed her back against the wall, breathing heavily, and stared at Frog. He was still alive but hurt and seemed unable to stand. Rage began to rise within her, and she slid her hand into her pocket and closed her fingers around her recharged battery.

As soon as the magic built in her veins, she whirled out from behind the wall and released blasts of purple magic from her fingertips as if they were guns. The energy swirled to form a hailstorm of magical bullets that struck three of the men behind the leader to drop them almost instantaneously. She rolled across the hard ground and ignored Lars's calls to her to get down.

One of the gang members raced toward her from the side, ready to grab her. She flipped her hand in the air and narrowed her glowing eyes. A pipe launched from one of the reconstruction sites nearby into her hand. She pitched her arm and caught the man in the side of the head.

Another immediately took his place. Her purple eyes shifted angrily to him and her top lip trembled like an angry dog showing its teeth. She bent slightly, vaulted upward, and spun her leg to kick him in the throat. He stumbled and grabbed at his neck as she landed. Stephanie stared at him for a moment and her eyes flickered to black. Her thoughts zeroed in on the man as rage and protectiveness lashed through her.

Slowly, she walked toward him, her gaze fixed and hard. His eyes widened when he saw the black orbs where her eyes should have been. She snatched him by the hair and dragged his head back before she whaled the pipe into his ribs over and over. The man coughed and spattered her face with blood. She growled angrily and flung him violently into the side of a half-fallen brick wall.

Lars continued the fight and fired relentlessly at any targets he could eliminate. All Stephanie could think about was revenge, her past, and her ancestor's past that connected with her in the present, just like it had been when Earth had once understood magic.

One thug remained. He stood in the street and tried desperately to replace the magazine in his gun. Stephanie threw the pipe down as she walked toward him and pushed her sleeves up. She pulled her palms together in front of her chest and turned them in a circular motion to form a ball of magic in her hands.

She looked slowly at him, growled, and launched the energy ball into him like a basketball pass. It erupted in his chest, lifted him from the ground, and spun him horizontally until the crumbled old brownstone across the street stopped him. The sound of cops arriving shook her from her connection. Her eyes faded from black to normal and she took a deep breath and pushed the magic in her into the ground.

"Stephanie," Lars yelled.

She turned and raced toward Frog, who lay motionless. Two of the gang members managed to make it to their feet. Stephanie knelt beside Frog and raised her hand to stop their assailants. Lars grabbed her wrist and shook his head. "That's enough. The cops will need to take it from here. It's best you don't use magic."

Stephanie swallowed and nodded in understanding. Her head swam slightly as she looked at Frog and placed her hand over a wound on his shoulder. Blood spewed down his chest and he groaned and writhed in pain. A cop ran up and looked at the downed gang members and then at Stephanie, whom he obviously recognized.

He holstered his gun and knelt to feel Frog's pulse. "I have an ambulance en route."

All she could do was hope that they could help her bodyguard before it was too late.

CHAPTER FOURTEEN

The blue padded chair in the corner of Frog's hospital room was horrendously uncomfortable. Stephanie sat with her feet pulled up and her knees to her chest. Her eyes remained fixed on the man in the bed while she waited and watched for him to become conscious again. The ambulance had been quick to get there, but he'd passed out on the way to the hospital. It was the downtown DC hospital but run by the Federation. Healthcare, at that point—unless you could afford a private doctor—was identical to that which the military received. Very surgical, emotionless, and understaffed.

She couldn't believe that something like that had happened. All she had wanted was a little time to be normal, but normal didn't seem to be an option for her anymore. Not to mention the kind of blank rage she had somehow disappeared into while the battle raged. She was fairly sure one of those who received a wrench to the face was in a room across the hall, guarded by Federation cops.

It was crazy. She'd known Frog for all of two days but had managed to bust his balls and get him shot. Apparently, being friends with her wasn't all that it was made out to be. Unless you liked living in a constant state of worry, wonder, and not knowing if you would survive to the next day.

Elizabeth walked through the door and paused to study Stephanie, who didn't even look at her. She gritted her teeth and released a long, deep breath before she walked up and handed her a hot cup of coffee. "It's not Brazilian roast but it will pass for coffee at this point."

Stephanie's gaze drifted from Frog's monitor to the coffee. Slowly, she took the cup and lowered her feet to the floor. "Thanks."

The older woman bit the inside of her cheek and sat down beside her. She had never been very good at helping those who needed comfort, but she knew it was part of her job. "What happened out there?"

She didn't answer at first but finally, she sniffled and shrugged. "We walked along a street, away from the circle. I didn't pay much attention to where we were, and we ended up face to face with them. They recognized me immediately—something I was shocked by, to be honest. They said there was a price to bring me in alive. That they would have a good payday."

Elizabeth sipped her coffee and grimaced slightly. "From the stories we were told, you acted like a warrior out there. There was even something about you cracking one of them in the head with a pipe."

Stephanie didn't laugh with her companion's chuckle. "I simply wanted revenge. I put my hand up and it came to me."

The other woman raised an eyebrow. "Like what? Like Thor's hammer?"

She shook her head, her gaze fixed on nothing in particular. "Mjolnir was forged from the heat of a dying star. This was some metal pipe from one of the construction sites. I don't know...it was the first thing I thought of when the guys tried to drag me away. I fought and it was like I zoned in like never before.

Anyway, it's not like it did a lot of good. Frog took a shot before we could even react."

Elizabeth looked at the man and studied the heartbeat monitor, which jigged and jagged at a regular pace. "It's a hazard, but Frog knew that. He did his duty, and you should be proud of him for that."

Stephanie blinked for the first time since before the woman had walked in. "I am proud of him and thankful. But that doesn't take away the fact that he was hurt protecting me. It isn't right. Is Lars okay?"

Her companion gave her a comforting look and pushed a piece of hair fallen from her ponytail over her shoulder. "He's fine. A little bruised but that's all. He'll join us shortly. I made him get a brain scan to make sure everything was good. It probably came up empty."

Stephanie pressed her lips together but finally, she grunted and gave up the attempt. She giggled at the joke, then tilted her head back and rubbed her face. "God, this sucks. I know I asked for this, I know I did, but I'm starting to think I don't want to be special anymore."

Elizabeth laughed, leaned back, and crossed her legs. She cradled her coffee and stared off into the corner of the room. "It's funny how we all wished for something when life was simpler, and when we got it, everything became ten times more complicated. That's when we hiccup, backtrack, and kick ourselves for thinking we wanted all these things."

"You are preaching to the choir here, girl." Stephanie snorted as she sipped her coffee. "I should have wished for a spot at my parents' company and a decent house in the subs. But then, if I got that, I wouldn't have been satisfied."

The older woman nodded, slightly dazed. She blinked and drew in a deep breath to bring herself back to the present. "The thing is, though, no matter what you believe about the great beyond, fate, magic—any of it really—sometimes, what you want doesn't matter. Sometimes, the things waiting in the wings for you will be bigger than you, bigger than all of us, and you have to take it with a sense of grace, compassion, and a stiff upper lip."

Stephanie pouted her bottom lip. "I wish I could argue with you on that, but I have no data to back myself up."

Elizabeth chuckled and glanced around uneasily. *You sound like Burt.*

They both laughed for a minute and the sound trickled around the steady beeping of Frog's monitors. She put her cup down and looked at Stephanie. "You are Stephanie Morgana, the Federation's first human witch. Like it or not, you will always be important. And you can fight it all you want to, scream, claw, but in the end, you will need to learn to lead people because they will follow you. You won't have a say in that. And you may try to push them off and convince them not to, but they will still be there."

The girl's fixed and serious expression didn't change. Her eyes were locked on the foot of Frog's bed, her thoughts almost visible. Elizabeth curled the left side of her mouth and turned to retrieve her coffee. "It's important to remember that, Stephanie. You will be a leader, like it or not. Some of the people following will do it for good reasons, and some...well, simply because they are bat-shit crazy."

Stephanie shook her head. "Those bat-shit crazy ones will simply write me hate mail or stab voodoo dolls. They are the ones who will be capable of really big and really scary things. Scary as in putting my name out there so gang members hunt me down. And because of that—because of me—innocent people will be hurt."

Elizabeth shook her head. "You need to realize that bad things will happen, whether to you, to people close to you, or to people you don't even know. You need to accept that here and now because otherwise, it will always hold you back. Be thankful that he isn't dead. That is something to hold onto and celebrate. We are sitting here waiting for him to wake up, not sending him to the Federation burial services to expel his ashes out into space."

She knew Elizabeth was right although she didn't say anything. Frog was really lucky to be alive, but it still made her sick to her stomach to see him like that. The other woman finished her coffee and tossed the cup in the bin. "I am personally glad, no matter what, that you didn't kill anyone or get anyone killed. That could have a profound effect on someone, and I need you to stay open and receptive so that you can continue to grow stronger and wiser."

She slapped the girl's leg to catch her attention. "Do you hear what I'm saying? We have an opportunity here to see the danger and attack it head-on. We get to help you figure out how to be Stephanie Morgana, Earth's first human witch, and do it with the knowledge and know-how to protect the people you care about. The people who are the most important to you. Death looming over you when you are desperately trying to learn and grow can be something incredibly hard to do. Especially with you being so young and so withdrawn for so long from the things in this world."

Stephanie shrugged. "Not all of it, but my parents tried hard to give me as normal a childhood as possible. Now that I see what is ahead—or could be—I am glad they did that. A few years where I can remember being worried about nothing but classes, tests, friends, and exams."

Elizabeth could see the sadness in the girl's eyes. She put her arm out and pulled her into a side hug. "Come here. Believe it or not, I know how you feel. I may not be a witch, but I know what it's like to have other's lives in your hands and to have someone go down. It is hard, but I also understand how important it is to not allow yourself to brood about it."

The door to the room opened and both Stephanie and Elizabeth stood. The doctor, in his early sixties with white hair, a white Federation lab coat, and with clipboard in his hands, glanced at them. He pressed his lips together and greeted them kindly. They watched as he looked at the different stats on Frog's vitals, flipped through his file, and made a couple of notes. When he was done, he turned to them and closed the chart.

"He will be fine," the doctor said. "There were a couple of severe wounds, which we did some repair on. He'll have a nasty scar and nerve damage in his shoulder but with some physical therapy, he should be able to go back to what he was doing before this incident. Take it easy on him."

"Yeah," Frog groaned, and his hand groped at nothing.

They hurried over and Stephanie took his hand. "How are you feeling?"

He sniffed and grimaced as he shifted a little on his back. "Like fried frog legs, but alive. And amused at your conversation. Stephanie, get over it. Shit happens. Move on and stop having a pity party."

Her mouth dropped open. "I…you jerk. You were awake that whole time?"

Her companions laughed and Frog rubbed her shoulder. "Seriously, though, you were like Chuck Norris crazy out there. You should be proud. And Elizabeth?" She raised her eyebrows. "Take her back so she can't sit here and stare at me like this and drive herself crazy while she watches my pee drain into a bag hanging on the bed."

Elizabeth smirked and hauled Stephanie away with a firm hand on her arm. As they reached the door, the girl turned back for a moment. "Thanks, Frog."

He put his thumb up. "Send me a hot nurse. I think a sponge bath is in order."

They walked into the hallway where Lars waited with a bruise on his cheek, a skinned elbow, and a small scrape on his forehead. "Are you gals ready to get back? I could use some coffee and a good chill session."

Stephanie nodded and Elizabeth slipped him a wink and

gestured with her eyes toward Steph. They stopped at the nurse's station and Lars walked to one of the nurses, a nondescript woman in her fifties or so wearing orthopedic shoes. "Ma'am, I wanted to let you know that the guy in room seven-six-five, Frog, he has requested a bath. He happened to hint that he hoped you would be the one to give it to him."

She giggled, nodded, and snatched up a rubber glove. "We'll get him nice and clean."

Lars hurried to catch up with the women. "Everything is right in the world now."

Elizabeth rolled her eyes and pulled them both in the elevator. "It won't be when he figures out what you did."

As the elevator doors began to close, they heard Frog's furious protest. "Lars! You asshole!"

Even Stephanie couldn't hold back the laughter as the elevator moved to the docking bay where the car was parked. Despite his injuries, Lars remained vigilant. He moved so that the women were behind him and stood with his feet slightly apart and his hands loose and close to his pockets. He turned slightly to look at them and his gaze flashed to Elizabeth and then to Stephanie. "I know this is all really hard to understand right now."

Stephanie's gaze lifted to meet his when she realized he was talking to her. "I feel better now that we know he'll be okay."

Lars shook his head. "I'm talking about trying to figure out life now that you are destined for something way bigger than yourself."

Her eyes glistened as she held his gaze for a moment and then folded her arms in front of her and stared at the floor again. "I think I was naïve to think that being special would be all candy and rainbows—or in my case, blue flames and cleansing spells. I guess in a way, I didn't think I would actually ever become someone special to others. So why think about the negative, right? A daydream."

The elevator opened and they followed Elizabeth down the

walkway to the car. Stephanie and Lars got in the back and the older woman took the driver's seat. They headed out in silence and eased into the lines of traffic to head out of the city.

Elizabeth glanced in the rearview mirror and adjusted it slightly to see Stephanie's eyes. "We want you to understand that there will be a whole lot of really cool things that come along with a life for someone who is destined to rise above."

Lars nodded. "That's right. A whole lot of cool stuff. But at the same time, with the good comes the bad. That fight won't be the last. Frog's injury won't be the last. What's important here is that you decide how you want to use your gifts. What path you want to take."

Elizabeth took the exit out of the downtown area. "Exactly, and then we can all follow that path because we believe in you. But you have to be ready for days like today. Even days ten times worse than this. You have to take this seriously. You have the talent to kick major ass, make huge differences, and sweep the Federation, but you have to believe in it."

Stephanie twisted her hands back and forth in her lap before her gaze met Elizabeth's in the mirror. "I got it. I…won't forget it either. Tomorrow, we start over."

Lars clapped his hands with a smile. "Whoop. That's damn right. And we get bragging rights 'cause we kicked some gang members' butts while the slackers were standing around the base twiddling their cheeky bits."

Stephanie looked at Lars and chuckled as she shook her head. "You guys have some issues."

Lars nodded. "Yep. And that's what makes us a really good team."

When they reached the compound, Lars headed to his quarters and Stephanie shuffled off to hers, obviously exhausted and with a lot of things to think about. Elizabeth checked the security logs and reported to the others that they were back. As she walked past the kitchen on her way to her room, she grabbed a glass and a bottle of red wine from the cabinet.

She hurried into her room and kicked her heels off, untucked her shirt, and sighed as she sank into her large fluffy armchair. As she drew the cork from the bottle, she inhaled a deep breath. "Oh, hello there, relaxation."

"I don't know how relaxing I will be," Burt said through the comms over her head.

Elizabeth winced and almost spilled the wine. "Good Lord. Didn't anyone ever teach you to not be a nasty creepy stalker?"

He paused but didn't answer the question. "I thought we might want to discuss providing a protection detail for her parents."

She took a big swig of her wine before she retrieved her tablet and clicked it on. In a moment, she'd selected an email and forwarded it to his email address. "I already took care of it—I had some buddies in Chicago looking for work. Her parents have a detail, but they won't know it. I also placed two guards in line for hiring with the company to keep an eye out when they are working there at night. That way, they can be right there in case of anything unexpected."

Burt scanned the email. "Good work. I knew my data was right when it said to hire you."

Elizabeth raised her glass and took a sip as she rolled her eyes. "Lucky me."

CHAPTER FIFTEEN

The ambassador sat in the study of his hotel suite and leaned back at the large mahogany desk. A vintage Tiffany lamp glowed softly as the sound of melodic tones played from the virtual tuner disk placed in the center of the workspace. Seemingly floating to his right was the next page of the most recent negotiation with different sections highlighted.

He read another line and reviewed both the Meligornian and English translations of it while a small holographic Meligornian dancer cascaded across the wooden surface doing a traditional gambol. A frame sat to the right, a small girl with a similar complexion and hair color to the dancer, and she giggled and danced on a continuous loop of a small stored memory.

Ambassador V'ritan swiped the page away and brought the next up. The song changed and he tilted his head to focus on the dancer as she glided across the surface in front of him. The memory in the frame changed as well. The little girl was now a woman, the same as the hologram dancing on the desk. The movements were identical, the swing of the arms fluid, and the smile bright and shining. As he watched, his eyelids lowered slightly, and a small tear built in the corner of his eye.

A sudden and loud knock on the door made V'ritan jump and he swiped the hologram away. He leaned across and snatched up the frame as he called out, "Just a moment."

His gazed fixed on the picture for a second before he drew his hand across it. A thin line of purple energy streamed from the center up to his temple. The air hissed through his nose as his body tightened and then relaxed. The frame now looked like nothing abnormal, a picture of his daughter with the words, "Ritutius Hartstrom Tia Shaerium." It meant, "Rest Easy, Little Star."

The ambassador replaced the frame on his desk, wiped the tear from the corner of his eye, and leaned his head on his fist, his elbow propped on the desk. He focused his sight on the papers in front of him. "Come in."

Brilgus opened the door, hurried in, and closed it behind him. He held a tablet in his hand and set it down carefully before he slid it across to him. The ambassador raised an eyebrow and looked at the device. "I thought I said that I wanted to not be disturbed today with inconsequential things, Brilgus."

The bodyguard lowered his head, his hands behind his back. "Of course, Ambassador. Although I thought you would want to read this update sent over only a few minutes ago."

The ambassador pursed his lips, sighed, and swiped his hand over the tablet. An email rose in holographic form and hovered in front of him. As he read, his muscles tensed, and his face shifted from irritation to worry. He looked quickly at Brilgus. "And she is all right?"

His guard nodded. "We had no one from our camp with her. It was only her and two of her bodyguards. They all, except her, sustained injuries. One is in the hospital and the other has been discharged."

V'ritan shook his head and pressed his finger to the attachments. Brilgus placed his fingers on the top and bottom corners and pulled out to make the video screen larger. "This was footage caught by Federation cameras that are placed throughout the city. It does not have audio, but I think it's self-explanatory."

The ambassador nodded and played the footage. He watched the battle rage on the screen and winced and turned his head several times as Stephanie used the pipe to beat the assailants. She grasped one of the men by the top of his head and turned hers toward the camera for barely a moment. He paused the video quickly and tilted his head to focus on the screen.

Brilgus followed suit and both reveled in her appearance. "Are her eyes completely black?"

The ambassador nodded his head but didn't speak. He pressed play again as an uneasiness stirred in his chest. When the battle was over, he leaned back and rubbed his chin. Brilgus pressed fast forward and then paused it. "That isn't it. There is something else on this video that perplexes me greatly."

V'ritan waved his hand and the other man pressed play. The emergency medics carried the guard away on a stretcher, his shoulder bloody and arm limp. That view of the street then remained empty for around twenty seconds before Stephanie walked into view again. She seemed to be perplexed and paced for a moment before she stopped and turned to face them. Very slowly, she withdrew her battery from her pocket and gazed at it. Suddenly, her head jerked up and she stared directly at the camera. A wisp of purple energy flickered in her pupils and then dissipated.

The guard paused it. "There. The battery."

The ambassador straightened and pressed the image to enhance the item she held in her hand. "Definitely a battery, but —wait."

Brilgus bit the inside of his cheek. "I thought there was another one too, but you would be able to see it outlined in her pockets. It now seems to be completely full, but that had to have been her only source."

V'ritan pushed quickly from his chair and walked around the

desk. He paced back and forth for several moments before he stopped and pointed at the frozen image. "That battery *is* full…it cannot be possible. How in the world did she have that much power to use? Assuming it was of high quality and full strength, that stone would be no more than a third full after that battle. And if it weren't high-end, it would practically be empty."

The other man wrinkled his nose and leaned forward toward the screen. "But it's not. It's full like she never touched it."

The ambassador shook his hand and his head simultaneously. "That is not possible. She has never even been to Meligorn other than during her pod simulations. She wouldn't have a way to store the energy, even if she could accomplish that without blowing herself to pieces. But then again, the proof is right there. She did do it, regardless of what science or common sense has to say about it."

Brilgus smirked at the screen. "I have to admit, I don't know how she does any of this. But she definitely has the form and technique down and is way more powerful than I thought she would be. She is possibly the strongest Earth witch that I have ever seen or read about. I am perplexed."

The Meligornian sighed, scratched his chin, and his eyes glazed over. "Me too, Brilgus. Me too."

***

Todd tapped his hands on the edge of the recruiter's desk as he waited for her to come out of her meeting. He had been picked up at home that morning by one of the recruiter cars and brought to the navy station to take his tests. For the first time in his life, he actually did some research, took a couple of practice exams online, and even combed his hair. It was a whole new world for him, but he wanted to make a good impression.

"Toddster," one of the other recruiters said and patted him on the shoulder as he passed. "Did you take your tests yet?"

He pointed downward. "That's what I'm here for. I'm gonna knock them out of the water."

The recruiter smiled with enthusiasm. "Yes, you are. Good luck, man. I'm off to pick up some new recruits and take them to the TRAM to catch their ride to boot camp."

Todd nodded enthusiastically as the man left. He immediately jumped to his feet as his recruiter approached. She gave him a kind smile and stuck her hand out. "Todd. Sorry that took so long. I wanted to make sure that everything was set up for you correctly."

He gestured airily. "Hey, no problem. I never care about waiting for friends."

She glanced at him and chuckled breathlessly. Hannah was really good at her job, crossed all her t's, and dotted all her i's. She was always friendly to the recruits because she knew that there would be a very large portion of them who would go in and not come back. At the same time, she had to be businesslike. It was what landed her that duty station, made her second highest recruiter in the office, and allowed her to cross through the military ranks without really raising any concerns or ruffling any feathers. But Todd was a teenage boy. He had raging hormones and weird ideas about what constituted a friend. He also stared at her ass on a regular basis like he somehow believed she wouldn't notice.

Todd thought she was really nice, and he hadn't stopped telling his friends about her since she'd contacted him. He truly thought he had made a friend. "Hey, did you ever watch that movie I told you about?"

Hannah glanced up. "Oh, uh...*Jumping Jack Flash?* I haven't had time yet but it's on my list for sure."

"If you want, I have it downloaded. You can come watch it on Saturday," he offered.

She cleared her throat and gave him a flat-lipped smile. "That's a really cool offer but I...um, I have to do some military stuff on Saturday. You know, keep up with the rat race over here."

Todd nodded and honestly didn't think anything of it. Hannah was glad he didn't push the subject. He was a cool kid and all, but she was there to get him signed in, not to become his bestie. She handled it with professionalism. It wasn't like it was the first time it had happened. She was a young, beautiful Latino woman with crazy blue eyes and a tight uniform. The boys tended to flock to her, not to mention the fact that she was kind to them or, at least, came off that way.

He smoothed his hair back and pulled down on his button-up. "So I'm taking all the remaining tests, right?"

Hannah put down her stack of papers. "Yep. I'll get you plugged in right now. It shouldn't take you very long. Honestly, it's not rocket science. Well, some of it is, but the rest will be a fly-by for you."

She led him to one of the testing rooms and hooked him up to the VR headsets they used for the placement testing. Exactly like the tests had been for decades, they were mostly multiple choice with a couple of short-answer questions thrown in.

Todd went directly to work and answered everything with ease. He was more than glad he had actually prepared and vaguely considered the possibility that if he had done that all along, he might have achieved better grades in school. Then again, he didn't really care about all that at the time. He'd simply wanted to download music and movies and hang out with Stephanie.

When he had completed the testing, he removed the headset and submitted them. He meandered back to where Hannah waited for him with a Federation Navy ballcap. "The computer is calculating your scores. When they are done, I will go over the info with my CO and give you a call to set up the rest of the process."

He smiled broadly and stood up tall with pride. "Thank you, Hannah. I can't wait!"

She chuckled and showed him to the door. "Jump in one of the cars out front and they'll take you home. And good luck on the last leg of school you have."

Todd walked out of the door and pulled his hat on, feeling like a new man. Hannah raised an eyebrow and closed the door before she returned to her desk. She pulled up the assessment page and leaned her head back against the chair to wait for the last score to come through. With all the technology available, she still couldn't understand why they had such archaic shit in the recruiting offices. But then again, it didn't really matter because unless a kid failed—which was damn near impossible—they put them wherever they wanted to anyway.

Hannah printed out the test scores, walked to her CO's office, and knocked on the door frame. He looked up and waved her in. "Petty Officer Santino, come in. How is the new recruit coming along?"

She handed him the scores. "Really well, actually. He tested in the top percent for aptitude. It surprised me, I won't lie. With his high school transcript, I didn't expect very much."

Captain Cromwell scanned the paper and narrowed his eyes. "Hmm, yes. He did do well. Although this seems to be a regular thing with your recruits—the male ones anyway. I have a feeling they are trying to impress you. You might have missed your calling as a teacher. Shaping bright minds one tight skirt at a time."

Hannah chuckled. "No, I don't think that would work. Besides, you know how I feel about kids. They're great when they are ready to enlist, sir. Snot-nosed, loud, and sticky when they are under eighteen."

Cromwell laughed deep and low. "This is why I like you, Santino. You always say it straight but in a tone that would make me think you were a saint. Luckily for the Federation, you aren't, and your three-year tour on the Abdunnasir in deep space showed that."

She put her hands behind her back and straightened. "I simply did my duty, sir. Those Dreth pirates were getting out of hand and someone needed to send them spiraling back into hell. But it was a team effort."

The captain smirked, his attention still on the papers. "And modest too. If all recruits were as good as you, we'd be one hell of a Federation Navy, wouldn't we? As it is, this kid shows promise. He could be good with Naval Intelligence."

Hannah nodded. "Yes, sir. That was my first thought."

The captain flipped the page to his physical stats. He snarled slightly. "We have to work on his physical attributes a little but nothing a diet and several dozen laps around the space track with higher gravitational pull won't fix. Get him set up. Good work."

She took the papers. "Oh. Also, he can feel the MU energy."

CHAPTER SIXTEEN

>>**R**eplay video from Wednesday, 4:33 pm, 1500 block of Church St. NW

BURT wanted to review the footage himself, knowing that one of his hires had been severely injured and that the other guard and Stephanie were somehow able to fight off almost a dozen men. It didn't compute for him that she would have been strong enough to do that yet in the real world. His system went through the video footage data and recreated the incident in a computational annalistic form that BURT quickly ran through his system. She fought the whole time using a mixture of magic and human emotion to fuel her skills.

>>**Query: Human capabilities without magic in Earth-based street fight.**

The computations were quick and easy and showed that even the most trained fighters would not be able to use the types of functional fighting moves she'd used in that capacity while also draining energy to use magic as well. Their average fight time would calculate to only seven minutes. She'd fought the gang members for over double that amount of time and did not need recovery afterward.

BURT replayed the video again and located the scene at the very end with the battery. From his calculations of both pixel saturation and form of object, the battery was almost completely full. According to his numbers, it should have been at least three-quarters empty, if not totally tapped. There were also no other signs of any other batteries on her person or disposed of during the fight. This left him perplexed.

"Could her Meligorn energy be adding something?" he asked himself as he continued to run through the data over and over, using caveats such as adrenaline and dietary intake to make the number make sense.

Despite his efforts, nothing emerged that brought any clarity. It was as if she did something with the energy conversion that he didn't understand. He was programmed with every byte of data on Earth, and if it were new and not yet uploaded, he could easily search for it through his connection with the Net servers. But no answer came in, which meant whatever was happening had not happened before in a way noticeable to mankind.

Stephanie whistled cheerfully as she hung her clothes up and walked to the pod. She was thankful that they were able to turn the heat up in the room. She had been freezing every time she went in and out. The pod regulated her temperature while inside, but the exit and entrance were not only awkward due to nudity but uncomfortable too.

She climbed into the pod, pulled the door shut, and lay back on the seat. The process had become seamless, and she rarely even noticed her switch from her human perception to when her avatar awoke in the virtual world. She opened her virtual eyes and glanced around at a Meligorn temple of sorts—not religious in nature like the ones on Earth but more focused on the magic of the world than anything else.

The dust puffed gently off the floor from the slide of her boots as she walked forward. The walls were all etched with a language she had never seen and in the center stood a pedestal with a small bowl on top. She approached cautiously and stared down at it. The liquid in the bowl wasn't water but wasn't something she recognized either. She narrowed her eyes and looked closer. Within the bowl, images played like an old movie but with people of Meligorn in the very temple in which she stood.

"That is the Mnemonic Basin," the voice of her Meligornian teacher, M'rick, said.

Stephanie looked up as he came gently down the steps to the right. "And what is it for?"

He put his arms out to the sides. "This is the Temple of Presage, located on Meligorn outside the Capital Burghal of Nastar. It is said that the temple was the first building ever to be erected and sits atop the very place that spills the magic from the core of the planet. It is thought to be the most mystical and magical place in the universe. That bowl was placed there on the day the last stone was set. No one filled it, and it filled itself with magic. Within the waves of the energy that you cannot feel with your hands, taste, or touch are the memories of every moment that has come to pass within these walls."

She looked back and attempted to touch the surface of the liquid. Her hand went right through as if it were a hologram. The faces that passed within the liquid changed and moved forward through time. It was fascinating, but she was still unsure of why she was there. She looked up at M'rick with a small frown.

He cracked a smile and chuckled. "You are wondering why you are here. It is an important place for both humans and Meligorn. And right now, I want to test you on your Meligorn magic absorption."

Stephanie, her forehead scrunched, shrugged her shoulders. "Why?"

M'rick smiled and led her to the open space within the Temple's atrium. "Humor me."

She nodded, happy to trust his guidance. Calm and relaxed, she stood in the center of the stone floor, closed her eyes, and breathed deeply through her nose. She pulled the MU up from the ground exactly as she had done before. When she had drawn enough, she whipped it around her and allowed it to flow through her like a continuous stream connected to her very being. Her body glowed brightly as she moved her shoulders and arms to command the flow like a conductor directed the orchestra.

M'rick watched a moment before he touched her arm to break the concentration. She opened her eyes and instead of the energy retreating immediately, it took its time to flow slowly through her and into the ground. BURT watched the entire thing and calculated every change in her body at every moment. Not only did she pass this examination of sorts, but it was obvious she used the MU in a new way. But how?

He queried the system as rapidly as he could and pulled resources from every place he could. In the end, it made no difference. There was no available data to extrapolate the potential issues. Nothing to compare to or contrast with. With this new form of magical and energetic control, he couldn't help but wonder if she would once again explode. But this time, would it be in real life?

Several men sat in a penthouse apartment smoking cigars and sipping bourbon. The place was decorated in old-world charm. Large, deeply colored oriental rugs, earth-toned vases from the ashes of some of the most important ruins in history, and framed documents that held both rich historical value and magical significance. One of the men, with dark hair, deep-set eyes, and a shadowed aura deepening his features, ran his finger over the edge of his rocks glass. He rolled his shoulders and the leather of his jacket made an uncomfortable creaking sound.

He looked at the three men across from him, all of them similarly dressed and very close in looks and prominent in stature. "What do they say on the ground?"

The man to his right—the one they called Beta P for the radioactive scars across his face and hands—sniffed and put his glass down. "The cut-out gangs were a failure."

The man beside him scoffed, uncrossed his legs, and tapped his cigar in the ashtray. "Like we thought they would be in the first place. They were pigs, low-level people who normally steal from the neighbor's cookie jar. Did you expect them to be capable of taking a human witch? It was a waste of time from the beginning and only made restrictions tighter."

"We had to start somewhere," another man pointed out. "It would have been better to snatch her quietly, but we now know that amateurs are not the way to solve this. She shouldn't be that powerful, not yet. Not with the small amount of energy she carried in her pocket. But we saw that it didn't matter how much she carried. Her powers are beyond what we fully understand."

Beta P rubbed his right hand abstractedly. The pain from his past radioactive injuries haunted him constantly. "Right. Well, now we know. And we need to make sure that we give her more focus with better quality outsourcing agents."

The main man maintained an expressionless face. "And the agents who hired the gang?"

Beta waved his hand dismissively and picked his drink up. "They are taken care of. They won't sing to anyone anytime soon. They knew the cost of failure and decided to use amateurs. Sadly, they paid for that mistake."

"What about her parents? They are the most important people to her," the man in the middle ventured.

The leader licked his lips and puffed at his cigar. "I think that at this time, with her powers unknown, we should leave the parents as a last resort. That kind of rage could create a backlash we aren't ready to handle. Besides, we would prefer to talk to her and foster her support for us and the cause. I don't think kidnapping the people she loves the most will put her in the mood to discuss anything other than our deaths."

They all could agree that they wanted her for more than simply her magic, her clout, her persuasion, and her intellect. They couldn't ever expect her to trust anything they said if they harmed the people she loved. It was not the way they usually handled business, but for her, they would agree on a softer form of advancement.

He smacked his mouth and the smoke billowed around the room. "So it's decided. We will work with more qualified agents to bring this girl in. Beta, I can assume you will get on top of this."

The man nodded. "Yes. I will make some calls as soon as we leave here."

The leader smashed his cigar down into his ashtray and set it on the table. He grunted slightly as he stood and walked to the balcony doors. With a sigh, he cracked them and watched absently as the smoke flooded out of the condo. That done, he walked to the bar, grabbed a napkin, and picked several olives up before he rested on a stool.

The other men waited for him to speak, knowing he had the agenda in his mind. He put an olive in his mouth and chewed. "What about the ambassador? I've seen nothing to suggest that he is on our priority list."

Beta glanced at the others, who seemed to like to stay quiet unless they thought they might be in line for recognition. "I have watched him in recent days in an effort to keep up with the girl and him, and I believe that we should ramp up our efforts when it comes to…clearing his voice."

The leader's gaze studied Beta as he popped another olive in his mouth. "Why is that?"

The man pursed his lips and considered his answer for a moment. "He, in my opinion, has too much success and influence in the Federation activities at the moment. It is becoming a liability that I'm not sure we need or want right now. There is a plan—a bigger one than any of these small things—but he has the ability to influence and change the course of Federation focus. Which you know, of course, is far from the direction in which we hope to go."

Although he grumbled under his breath, the leader nodded his head as he wiped his fingers. "Yes. I've seen the amount of travel and the new agreements put forward between nations recently. It definitely has the potential to dampen our efforts. We all should know that the most important part that we need to watch here—continually watch—is the Federation's efforts with the Dreth pirates. The harsher they seem, the more their ships will be pointed at the Dreth's throats. The more they chase them off into deep space, the less their focus will look behind or to the side. We have known for a long time that the Federation works with blinders on. They assume that they can somehow protect themselves from all angles of space. This is absurd, of course."

The three men nodded. "Of course. Absurd."

He walked back to his chair and sat. "It is vital that we keep the pirates as the focal point for the Federation, NorAm, and everyone else, for that matter. Anyone who could spook the Federation should be contained. Their heads need to be forcefully turned toward the Dreth pirate ships. We do not want anyone—the Federation, Dreth, or Meligorn—to see what is going on behind the scenes until it is so far gone that there will be nothing they can do to stop it."

Beta mumbled and flexed his fist. "And the ambassador is one of those beings who could quickly throw this whole thing off course. With his voice in the public and political arena, as well as the well-documented Meligorn intelligence, he is probably the most dangerous individual to us in the whole universe. God knows the Dreth and their tiny pea-brains are no threat. They can barely get full sentences out or ships off the surface, much less figure things out."

The leader chuckled and wiped his nose on the back of his hand. "True, Beta, and your passion shows your true heart in this matter. So we need to get close to the ambassador. What are your suggestions for this? And you two need to start putting your brains to use. I am not here simply to make you feel important."

The other two men cleared their throats and straightened, slightly wounded. The third man shrugged his shoulders. "We could go wherever he has dinner or a social event. It can't be hard to hack into his schedule."

Beta groaned. "His schedule is kept by letter magic and only absorbed by himself and his half-breed guard, Brilgus. Unless you have Meligornian magical abilities, I don't see that being an option."

The man in the middle leaned forward. "What if we were to wait outside his hotel and simply take him?"

Everyone looked at him silently for a moment. The leader raised an eyebrow. "And you have discovered the secret to blocking Meligornian magic from the highest non-royal in Meligorn. That is fantastic, but why have you hidden it from us all this time?"

He pursed his lips and his gaze broke contact with the leader. Beta rubbed the side of his face. "In all reality, the best option for us at this time would be to determine how to use one of those individuals within his support team. Their schedules are easy to find, there are humans without powers within the ranks, and they don't travel with protection. Most of them are young, too—interns and fresh prep school graduates taking positions to work up in the Federation graces. They are often naïve and careless with their safety precautions. It shouldn't be too hard to get to them."

The leader thought about it for a moment. "That does seem to be one of our only choices at the moment. What if we cannot get one of them to agree?"

Beta shrugged. "Then we dispose of one and put one of ours in their place. This would allow for a more secretive movement and keep anyone from blowing the whistle on the whole thing. Getting in touch with someone who can do this has never been a problem, but we have found little reason for it…until now."

CHAPTER SEVENTEEN

Lars chuckled as he walked down the hallway with the rest of the team in tow. Brenden was recounting his night out on the town with some girl he had met while shopping at the market. She was apparently some sort of intern working with the ambassador's team.

"She actually said to me that she hoped that they would one day build a shrine to Meligorn, maybe in the place of the White House. I asked her why we would do that here and she told me because Meligorn will be our savior. I tried to keep a straight face, but I was frankly terrible at it. She almost knocked me out of my chair. And that, sadly, was where the date ended."

Avery scoffed. "Sadly? You were still interested after that?"

Brenden shrugged. "No one cares about her weird obsession with the other planet when she is face down in my be—"

Elizabeth stepped out in front of them and Brenden cut short and cleared his throat. Her gaze darted from one to the other with a strange smirk on her lips. "Morning, fellas. Off for some more torture?"

Johnny snorted. "We have a thing for pain, apparently."

Marcus put his hands up and shook his head. "Nah ah. You have a thing for pain. I'm here because Lars threatened me and… well, I don't really want to know if he would actually follow through. So I am taking my chances with Steph. She seems to have a little more mercy."

Lars raised an eyebrow and chuckled. "We'll see about that. We might have to get her out of bed. We'll send you, Marcus, since you see the softer side of her."

Marcus wrinkled his nose. "Man, you are taking this lead position too far. Mrs. E, please reprimand him."

She popped an almond in her mouth and chuckled. "Call me Elizabeth, please, not Mrs. Anything. No ring on this finger, sir. I have too many men around me all the time as it is. I don't want to have to be forced to be nice to you out of contractual obligation."

He saluted her and she shook her head and stepped to the side. "Have fun, work hard, and if you need to get her up, put it into the system for her AI. That way, she doesn't chop you in the throat. The AI is safe."

They all continued down the hall to the training room. As they walked in, those in front turned and shushed them. Stephanie stood on the mats, her eyes closed, her right knee bent and her foot resting on the left, and her palms pressed together high over her head. It was not normal in the least for her to be up and working out early, and especially not the first one there. They all stood and simply watched as her attention never wavered. It was as if they had never stepped into the room.

Stephanie practiced her katas with perfect precision, every movement deliberate and every shift sharp and swift. She initiated the routine with the Shotokan Kihon Kata, beginning in the ready stance. Slowly, she turned left, kept her feet in the left front stance, and quickly thrust her arm downward into a block. From there, she stepped forward into a right front stance, lunged, and punched through the center. Her body turned to the right in a fluid motion as she used her forearm to throw a right downward block.

As she continued, she danced lightly on her feet and moved with resolution. She neared the end of her kata and turned right one hundred and eighty degrees. Her left foot moved slightly forward, and she used her right forearm again to block. From there, she took a deliberate step forward and called out as she punched with her left arm down the middle. Her body snapped back into a ready stance and she brought her palms together at her chest. She bent forward, bowed, and paused a moment before she straightened and opened her eyes.

Lars glanced at the others and hastily made eye contact. No one needed to say a word. They all knew what was happening. Her guilt drove her to perfection, an admirable thought but also dangerous in context. The men dropped their things and walked onto the mat to surround her in a loving way.

Marcus put his hand on her shoulder, but her stare didn't shift. "There is no need to feel guilty. You were more than part of the team out there. We are so grateful that no one was hurt any worse. This is not the first stay in the hospital for Frog, and it won't be the last. We know these things are possible."

Lars threw out a correction. "Probable."

Marcus nodded. "That's right. Probable. But we do it for our jobs and for the people we care about."

Stephanie breathed in deeply and let the air out slowly. She touched Marcus's hand before she turned to the others. "Guilt or no guilt, it doesn't change the fact that if I can't help protect myself, more people will be harmed and possibly killed. Even a scratch on one of us, in my eyes, is a reason to train harder, work more, and attain an even higher understanding of what it means to protect."

Johnny shook his head. "But you aren't alone. You don't have to do it on your own."

She looked at him with a slight smile for a moment before she shifted her gaze to her hands. "All my life, I knew that there was something different about me, even if I had no proof. If my life needs protection, I will not allow those voluntarily doing it to fight on their own. I am not the king of the chessboard, the piece to always be protected."

Lars scrunched his brow. "In a way, though, you are. Your capabilities are so far beyond anyone's understanding and your ability to change things is worth the scratches, holes in our arms, and yes, even death. One life for many. That is a no brainer."

Stephanie put her hand on his shoulder and turned to speak to everyone. "While I feel I shouldn't be the king, I do consider myself the queen. And everyone—anyone—who attacks my people will feel my wrath. If you will protect me for the betterment of all mankind, then I will use my powers to make sure you don't die doing it. And if you are hurt, we will avenge that pain. We will strike and I will not stand unseen in the shadows. I will walk in front of you, leading like I should."

The guys all nodded and felt the power that radiated from her. Stephanie had impressed them with her mature and loving thoughts. She brought them closer to an understanding that it wasn't merely a job that would pay the bills. They were part of something bigger than all of them. In that moment, as the sun began to rise outside and the world began to wake, Stephanie no longer had guards or employees. Now, for better or worse, gash or death, she began to assemble her army of followers.

Marcus turned his body to the side and grabbed Stephanie's wrist as she threw a hard punch at his chest. Immediately, he stepped back and yanked her off balance. He grabbed her shoulder swiftly with his other hand and hauled her into him as he thrust his knee into her stomach. As soon as she doubled over to grab her belly, he ground his elbow between her shoulder blades and knocked her off her feet. She landed on her back and groaned before she rolled onto her side and coughed.

Elizabeth clapped and paced back and forth on the sidelines. "Pick it up, Steph. The enemy won't let you take a moment to gather your nuts after a blow like that. You gotta push it out and roll out of it. Remember—move, keep moving, don't stop moving. If it were me, I would kick you so hard right now you would instantly shit teeth. But if you hit the ground and roll, they will have a harder time dogpiling you."

Stephanie slapped her hand on the ground. Spit dripped from her lip as she pushed to her feet. She wiped her mouth on the back of her sleeve and shoved her mouthguard back into place. Elizabeth stepped back, folded her arms, and watched as Marcus attacked again.

The training room was always Elizabeth's favorite place to be. No matter what job she had going on, she could always put her focus on one thing in the gym and that was to continually hone her fighting skills. When she was younger, she had taken her fair share of beatings, but she'd always gotten back up and never complained, exactly like Stephanie. As she stood and watched the blocks, kicks, and punches, Elizabeth's mind fluttered back to her younger years.

She was a tall girl and had always been taller than everyone else. But she was strong, muscular, and lean and spent her whole childhood learning how to protect herself the best way she could. She grew up during the civil unrest of the late 2080s. It had started as a positive thing but grew into another reason for the poor to lash out in anger, be punished by the Federation, and lash out some more. She could remember the last day of the unrest so vividly in her mind.

The sirens had blared loudly throughout her Kentucky hometown. She had run outside to see what was happening. There had been a rally downtown, and her father had gone to try to speak peace to both sides. He was an advocate for freedom and separation from the Federation but used his time trying to sponsor conversation instead of fighting. He hadn't always been that way, but when Elizabeth was only a little girl, her mother had been beaten to death in the streets by rebels who had started to form the basis for the civil unrest. They thought she was a Federation undercover agent and were desperate to grab their attention. It was only when they were arrested and convicted by the Federation forces that they heard the truth and realized what they had done—that her mother was one of them.

Elizabeth knew the sound of gunfire all too well before lasers were used on a regular basis. She heard the shots the day the men were executed by bullets to the back of the head in the center of the town. And on that last day of civil unrest, as she stood at the end of her suburban driveway and looked out at the cityscape, she heard them again. This time, though, she knew before anyone told her that her father was gone.

From there, she began to train, did what she needed to do, lived in Gov-Sub housing, and listened to her aunt whenever she raged. But she fought hard and long, and by the time she reached Stephanie's age, she was able to protect herself better than anyone she knew. The passion of her father's glow drove every punch and kick, surged every string of anger, and cemented her purpose in life. Up until Burt, though, she hadn't even really tried.

Stephanie backflipped off Marcus's chest and landed lightly, bolted forward, and pounded him as hard as she could in the stomach. Elizabeth shook her memories away and clapped. "Good, very good."

She had come to see Stephanie as her protégé, much like her teacher, rebel warrior Alexander Sclovickia, now long since passed, had brought her under his wing. "Take five. Get some water."

She walked over to the bench where Stephanie toweled her head and guzzled water. "I hope you understand that I am pushing you like this for your own good."

The girl's gaze met hers as she swallowed her gulp of water. "I know. I get it."

Elizabeth sat beside her and sighed. "I can't protect you all the time, but I can teach you to know what is coming. Sometimes, that alone is key to winning a fight."

Stephanie smiled at her before she pushed up and pointed to Lars. "You're mine, butthead."

Elizabeth chuckled and leaned back against the wall. Her mind drifted again, but this time, she had gotten older, wiser, and caught up in things she really didn't fully grasp. She had to make money and she did it doing what she did best—finding people and sending them a message, usually with violence. There were a great many things that she had done when she was younger that she was not proud of. Deep down, she knew that was why she sat there day after day, watched Stephanie, and pushed her to be better. Pushed for her to do the right thing, not the easy one.

All those tiny little moments, the ones that imprint on your soul, had stayed buried for a long time. But she hoped that within all that dark and deceit there was a glimmer of light. A lesson learned that she could pass on to the young girl. There were always other options, and each person had to do what they thought was best. But sometimes, those options were really hard to see. Pride and fear drove the rest of it, the fight for the top and the terrifying thought that all their hard work would be completely wasted.

Stephanie yelled and drew her attention back to the floor. The girl flipped Lars over her back and thrust her hand forward to stop barely inches from his throat. They smiled at one another and Stephanie looked at Elizabeth, gave her a wink, and pointed at her with reverence.

Elizabeth chuckled and shook it off, acting like it was no big deal. She had to do that. She had to show separation. But what she really hoped she'd found in her relationship with Stephanie and all the others was so much simpler but so very difficult to attain.

Elizabeth simply wanted forgiveness.

CHAPTER EIGHTEEN

Stephanie stood in the pod room, her mood the same as it had been for the last several days. She was focused, her intentions clear, and she continued to push the anger and frustration she felt aside. The last several days had been busy. She woke at five in the morning, worked out hard with the guys, ate a healthy meal, had pod time until dinner, got a run in, and went to bed. Usually, she worked herself so hard during the day that she didn't have any problem falling asleep. But while she slept, her mind took her back to the fight. Over and over again, she stood to the side and watched like a spectator, viewing herself from the outside. She watched Frog go down and the entirety of her body shift into a mode that she hadn't been able to fully shake.

As far as the Virtual World went, she had mostly worked on real-world tactics—things she could use to interact with others but all in the comfort of Meligorn. At the end of each pod session, she would spend some time working on her theories. The silence was perfect for her but deafening even for BURT, who hadn't really spoken much. She wasn't sure what she was in for that day, but she didn't care as long as she moved forward. By this point, she no longer fought to play with magic like a child.

That child had jumped ship in the streets of DC as she beat a man with a pipe.

Stephanie entered the pod, closed the lid, and barely felt herself drift off thanks to the dulcet effects of the serum. When she opened her eyes, she stood in the avatar dressing room, somewhere she hadn't been for a while. She was usually already dressed and inside Meligorn. She looked around, unsure of why she was there.

After a few moments of silence, she glared upward into the infinite blackness of the space above her. "Hello? I don't need to indulge in fancy clothes. I simply need to get to my next spot."

Suddenly, a rack appeared in front of her and held several different armored body suits. The AI spoke around her. "Today's mission will be different. A game of sorts, to test the abilities you have thus far acquired. It will be tactically suited to your taste but understand that once in, you cannot reach out for other gear or protection. This is meant to be a real-world simulation. Choose your armor, boots, weapons, and backup ammo. The game will begin in three minutes."

A digital clock appeared on the wall and Stephanie stared at it for a moment as it began to tick backward, counting her down. She swung into action, swiped through the armor, and selected the one on the end. It was a tight black suit with chest, shoulder, and thigh protection. For her waist, she chose a small tactical belt and filled it with two hand laser guns and two backup cartridges. She then chose the largest battery and slid it into a small pouch on her leg. Her attempt at a second failed as the system only allowed one. She didn't care. Wherever she was, she knew she would be able to manipulate the energy for her use.

As she tapped her choice of boots and rocked back and forth on the soles, the clock reached 00:00 and the avatar creation program faded to black.

"Your game begins now," the AI instructed. "Your mission is to capture, disarm, or kill the Dreth pirates fighting your squadron.

Those on your team are your partners, avatars pulled from real-life soldiers of the Federation army and navy."

Stephanie scowled and grumbled under her breath. "What's the army doing in space?"

The AI didn't respond but continued her instruction. "Once the Dreth are all captured, the game will end. Try to keep all civilians safe in the process. Good luck."

That little snippet of information surprised her. "Civilians?"

The system sped around her and came to a halt inside some dark hallway. Soldiers raced around her, and gunfire and explosions echoed from outside the doors. A loud boom shook the building and she flailed for balance and rubbed her hand down the soot-covered wall. It was smooth and familiar. She withdrew her hand and saw the shiny white cinderblock beneath the layers of dirt and grime. There was something so familiar about it and she couldn't shake the odd feeling.

Suddenly, a hand grabbed her by the arm and spun her around. It was a navy officer, his helmet tight on his head. He raised the front and scowled. "Come on, soldier. Get it together. People are dying out there. Get a move on."

He slapped his visor shut and fell in behind a line of sailors and soldiers who ran toward a door to the outside at the end of the hall. Stephanie shook her head and ran after them. She ducked beneath a fallen beam as she stepped out of the dark and into the light of day. Her feet slowed almost immediately, and surprise took over.

This was not the peaceful rippling and majestic shores of Meligorn. It was not the ravaged and ruined post-apocalyptic rocky terrain of Dreth. It was Earth. And not simply anywhere on Earth. She stood planted on the same sidewalk where she used to stand with Todd talking about pop culture and math tests. The same school she had attended since she was a kid. It was war-torn and crumbling but still the same place.

Her surprise left her stunned, but only momentarily. A

streaking laser hissed past her face, singed a few pieces of hair, and brought her back to the war that unfolded around her. She looked up with wide eyes as the Dreth pirates raged, marched on the humans, and laid waste to what had already been considered a ghetto.

Stephanie gritted her teeth, slammed her hand on the battery, and drew the energy from it. She twisted her hands to create a whirling purple orb. As the energy built, she moved her feet again, this time at a quickened pace as she hurtled toward one of the Dreth. She continued to manipulate her hands to grow the orb until finally, she was close enough to take a shot. Her eyes narrowed in concentration, she released her magical weapon with her full strength behind the throw to deliver a punishing strike to the pirate. She continued to run as she drew more energy. Up ahead was a pile of rubble with a platform on top. She sprinted faster and used some of the magic to launch herself up the side. As her feet found purchase on the platform, she released her magic and hundreds of small bullet-shaped pulses erupted into the massed battle that continued to rage.

Instinct reminded her not to remain in the open and she scrambled off the elevation and immediately broke into a run. A familiar voice yelled in pain and she slowed to turn her head right and left as panic rose in her throat. To her right, a guy lay on the ground, his hand up toward the Dreth who towered over him. Stephanie took a couple of steps closer and the helpless figure turned his head, his eyes hopeful.

Her lungs seized in her chest as she registered what everything in her refused to accept. Todd lay dying on the ground. She cupped her hands and drew in as much magic as she could. In mid-sprint, she released it in a single enormous ball that rocketed into the Dreth pirate about to stab Todd with a large, sharp sword. The attacker shrieked loudly and disintegrated in front of her. She hurried to Todd's side, helped him to his feet, and put her arm around his waist.

She knew it wasn't real, that it was only a simulation, but it was a perfect replica, even down to the smell of the cheap body spray he had always worn. Another Dreth pirate approached at a run with sharp teeth that dripped drool and a long golden pitchfork in his claw. Stephanie shoved Todd down on a pile of rubble and slapped her hand against her battery. There was no response. No feeling of energy, no feeling of magic, nothing. She fumbled in her pocket and drew it out in disbelief. The stone was cold and empty.

She rolled her eyes, threw it on the ground, and pushed her sleeves up. The pirate drew closer and closer, but she was determined to test her theory. She lowered her hands and focused on her senses, but nothing came except the enraged attacker. Time seemed to slow as she tried again and again before she finally drew her guns and fired directly into the Dreth's face.

The pirate's head fragmented, and his body slumped instantly. Angry, Stephanie thrust the guns into their holsters and stormed over to a large pile of rubble. She scrambled to the top and raised her hands. "Time out! Stop the game," she demanded harshly and assumed the AI would respond.

Everything froze. She lowered her hands and pursed her lips. After a few seconds, the AI spoke from above as if it came from the heavens. "You are not normally authorized to stop in mid-fight, but I was given the allowance this time. What can I do for you?"

Stephanie pointed at the ground where her battery lay. "This is not accurate. Just because I don't have a battery doesn't mean my magic stops."

The AI paused. "It does. The battery gives you what you need to begin, but there is no magic to collect on Earth. You must therefore use your human skills."

Stephanie shook her hand back and forth. "No, no, no. That is not how I work. I have been working on a theory—one that is backed by research and personal experience. There is energy here on Earth. It is similar to the energy and magic found on Meligorn but the problem is that humans don't know how to tap into it anymore. It's been lost for thousands of years, stamped out by a bunch of old rulers in the Middle Ages."

The AI responded in a monotone voice. "I am not familiar with this energy. It is not programmed into my system."

She sighed with real frustration. "Of course not. It is only referenced in the deepest parts of the net. The bigwigs don't want humans to know of this."

"How is it like the Meligornian magic?" the AI asked.

Her eyes narrowed as she tried to focus on the challenge. She would have to do her best to explain with limited knowledge. "Okay, so MU is a kind of energy that allows the user to twist it and bend it to their personal will. The scale here on Earth is the same, in essence, but instead of magical energy, it's light energy. It has different spectrums to it. The Earth spectrum is more refined and more powerful. At the same time, it is much harder to tap into. When you do, you could easily fry your circuits."

The AI didn't answer but the simulation remained frozen. Stephanie looked around, unsure as to whether the disembodied assistant was still present. "Hello?"

"Yes, sorry. I thought I might be better to discuss this matter with," Burt replied. "If what you are saying is correct, then there will be places in which this light energy is stronger or more abundant."

Stephanie licked her lips and clapped her hands, relieved that he had intruded and replaced the usual AI. "Yes. Yes. I thought about that too. I wondered if maybe it had to do with the significant places on Earth, like the Temple on Meligorn. Or perhaps geographical things like the equator."

He listened for a moment while he ran a search in the background for supernatural, magical, or strange locations. "What about ley lines?"

She thought about it for a moment and then nodded. "Sure,

uh…yeah, that could be something. Does it look like it could make a difference?"

BURT immediately began to calculate the major ley lines spoken about in the past. He ran the numbers, the occurrences, and the theories on them in record time but nothing was conclusive. "There are reported occurrences from time to time on the major ley lines, but nothing definitive. Nothing proven. There is no real logic to the existing ones that I can find."

Stephanie chewed her nail. "Damnit."

"But," he continued, "it doesn't rule out the theory behind it. Some of the places might need to be investigated and you would be the best candidate to do so. It would be difficult for anyone who wasn't connected to the magic to know if there was anything going on in those locations."

Stephanie nodded. "Right."

"That will be for a later review," he replied. "Tell me, does the energy feel the same as it does on Meligorn?"

Stephanie wrinkled her nose and thought about it. "It's hard to tell you what something feels like. The only time I have really utilized it on Earth was during the fight in DC. That whole thing happened in something of a fog, though. I went from battery directly into light—a seamless transition. But what I can say is that I would call it a three compared to Meligorn, which I'd put at a one on the scale and so top of the range. Earth power does not feel as strong but is still useable. I have a working theory on it, though. I've tested this theory through hand calculations each night on Earth."

BURT was impressed. "Excellent. What is the theory?"

She turned, scrambled down the rubble, and jumped the last few feet to the ground. "The theory is that as I get better with the use of the light magic and the Meligorn magic, I will be able to tap into it even more. Right now, there is a real danger to it, something that has to be watched carefully, especially on Earth. Here, if I die, I come back. There, if I die, I stay dead.

Opening myself to too much too fast could have catastrophic results."

"Then we will begin that research after this," he replied. "I have reprogrammed the system to have a likeliness of Meligornian magic but using your scale as you described it to be. It might not be perfect, but it's the only information we have on it. Either way, you will be able to use it in this scenario. I want to see how well it works. Let's resume the battle."

She assumed a ready stance, her hands at her sides as her fingers wiggled with anticipation.

CHAPTER NINETEEN

Stephanie put one hand down on the cement that halfway blocked the street and leapt over it. Her momentum didn't stop, and a mixture of adrenaline and the awareness of the light energy thrummed and pulsed in the background of her chest. She was careful with it and avoided overzealousness. Ahead and to her right, three soldiers battled a single Dreth. The pirate was strong, and they had run out of weaponry. Stephanie looked above her head and followed the electrical line to a large and very old oak tree directly behind the attacker.

The spark of magic flinted inside her with an odd pop and sizzle. She raised her arm and made a sharp gesture, A small flare of energy burst free and hissed into the electrical wire, which vibrated wildly as the pole swayed back and forth. She did it again, this time with more power. The cable writhed overhead and snapped to arc toward the oak. As the flashing and fiery end struck the tree, it immediately burst into flames. The blaze spilled over onto the Dreth pirate like a bucket of tar.

The soldiers looked at her and raced in her direction as the pirate stumbled crazily and ignited everything he touched before he finally succumbed to the flames. One of the soldiers shook her hand and pointed outward. "This is not the Dreth's doing. There are three others who have control over this battle. The pirates are paid mercenaries for them. Eliminate those three and this will end. The Dreth will either fight or surrender, but we will have the upper hand."

Stephanie turned her focus down the street and onto three operatives dressed in black suits with no real discernable features. They stood in a line but a short distance from one another and gestured at the different Dreth. She could see they were armed—and armed heavily.

Her mind made up, she slapped the soldier on the arm. "Got it. You and whoever else you can mobilize, get any civilians out of here and attack the Dreth. The more you can get rid of now, the less likely that there will be a revolt when the three men are dead."

The soldiers agreed and ran off in search of others. Stephanie sprinted toward the men. She deliberately chose a path down the center of the street and stared at them, unperturbed that they could see her. None of them drew their weapons, something she couldn't understand at all. They simply stood and watched her approach, their arms folded. She shrugged and continued. "Hey, when you aren't given a nose, a healthy complexion, or decent clothes as an avatar, I guess you don't give a rat's ass."

When she reached the cement roadblocks she'd passed earlier, she dove and twisted her body. Her feet cleared and she prepared to tuck and roll, but before she could pull her knees to her chest, a large hand encircled her chest. The stop jolted her momentum and her arms and legs flailed forward. Her head turned and she gasped at a large Dreth creature, light-brown from head to foot, with a huge bald head. It's arms, legs, and torso resembled a twisted tree nymph.

It hurled her to the ground, and she careened and rolled until she skidded into a motionless heap at the feet of one of the men. He looked angrily at her and yanked a half sword from a sheath on his back. From her sprawled vantage point, he appeared much larger than she'd expected. He held his sword at his eye level and his body tensed for the inevitable blow. As he thrust down, Stephanie dragged her energy up to form a shield. She focused all her strength into it and flinched when the metal impacted against the magic and hissed in violent response. Her attacker struggled to retain his hold on the weapon, but the force of the magic-infused barrier whipped it from his hand.

He gritted his teeth, snatched a piece of wood from the ground beside him, and resumed the offensive. As he swung his improvised weapon, Stephanie released the magic in her shield to create a fine dust in the palm of her hand. She rolled to the right and the rough timber struck the ground close to her head. Elizabeth's words echoed in her mind and she instantly rolled to the left to barely avoid a second blow. She rolled a third time, the man narrowed his eyes at her, and she smirked, opened her palm, and blew the dust into his eyes.

The operative screamed, dropped the board, and clutched his eyes with both hands. She pushed to her feet and shook her head. In seconds, she had drawn her leg back, grabbed his shoulders, and kneed him hard in the groin. A loud expletive replaced his screams and he doubled over. Stephanie snorted and turned, folded her arm, and elbowed him in the back of the neck. He collapsed face first, unconscious.

Running footsteps commanded her attention and she refocused on her adversaries. To her right, the second of the three men sprinted along a small ditch which contained shards of metal and plastic that protruded from the mud. To her left, another had already begun his attack, a knife in his hand. She thought fast. There was no way to take them both on at the same time. She swiped her hand to the right and the energy knocked that attacker's legs out from beneath him. His body attempted a twist to avoid the danger, but Stephanie gestured dramatically to create a wind that hurled him over the edge of the ditch and into the sharp metal.

She turned her head toward the last one, who had slowed down and now smirked and brandished his dagger menacingly. Unperturbed, she raised an eyebrow and flung her arm out to the left to release a massive blast of light energy from her fingers. It imploded against a large wooden crate mere feet from his ass. When the light struck the box, Stephanie dove behind a metal container a scant few feet away. The entire box blew and launched large shards of jagged wood in all directions with incredible force. The man didn't stand a chance and was instantly sliced like deli meat.

Stephanie clapped her hands in excitement and clambered onto the crate to assess the scene. The Dreth either immediately started to surrender or allowed themselves to be killed. The scenery around her began to fade and the system jolted her back to the avatar room.

"Congratulations, you successfully completed the simulation," the AI said. "Do you wish to end your pod session here or continue to another area of the Virtual World?"

She chuckled and enjoyed the excitement that still lingered. "End session."

"Thank you…good bye."

When her eyes open in the pod, the door released and allowed the light in. She stepped out and into the real world. Her fingers and the soles of her feet tingled wildly, and she couldn't help but smile at the feeling. That meant that her theory was accurate—the light energy was somehow searching for her. It knew she was the one to find.

She pulled her robe on and gathered her clothes before she opened the door. Before she closed it fully behind her, she looked back with a grin. She had done the right thing and actually won, all based on her theories and understanding. It felt really good.

Beta stood in the dark shadow of an alley and his cigar burned bright red at the end. He wore a large-brimmed hat and a long black trench coat, and black gloves covered his scarred hands. Three men waited with him—two on the other side, pressed against the damp brick wall, and one in front of him with a pair of binoculars to his eyes focused on the building catty-corner to them.

One of the men across from him checked his watch and nodded. "Why come all the way out here when you could have had us take care of this?"

He puffed his cigar and blew large rings of smoke over his head. He finally ended the short silence when he smacked his lips and looked at the cigar as he rolled it back and forth between his long, thick fingers. "Because the last idiots we sent to do a job hired someone else to do it, and they failed. Those agents are now spread in pieces throughout the city."

The man swallowed hard. "So you're here to take care of us if we fail."

A deep, nefarious grin pulled at his scarred lips. "No. I don't take the trash out. I'm here to make sure that failure doesn't happen. I'm tired of leaving things to chance. This should have been done a long time ago. I'm like your babysitter. I'm here to make sure that the girl—" He drew an imaginary line with his cigar. "That she gets into the freaking van. Simple."

The agent beside him put his binoculars down. "She just walked into the lobby of the apartment building."

Beta put his finger to his earpiece. "She's coming out. Get into position."

The team remained inconspicuous but watched as a small blonde girl dressed in a cocktail dress and carrying a small black purse walked quickly out of the complex. She glanced around her and turned right toward the sky rail entrance three blocks down. A large nondescript brown van crept along behind her and waited for her to move down a block where there were barely any people. As soon as she reached the mark, it sped up and came to a screeching halt beside her. Three men piled out of the vehicle, one with a black velvet bag, and the other two with their sheer strength.

The girl looked frightened in the split second before they shoved the bag over her head and grabbed her arms. They hauled her off her feet, threw her into the van, and scrambled in after her. One of them looked around and slid the door closed as the van accelerated down the street.

Beta put his finger to his earpiece. "Good. You know the plan from here."

He removed the device, dropped it on the ground, and tossed his cigar on top of it. With the flat of his shoe, he stepped down hard and twisted his foot in a crushing motion. Small red embers floated outward and sizzled in the dark puddles alongside. Satisfied that no obvious evidence remained, he pulled his phone from his pocket, pressed a button, and put it to his ear. "The girl is out of the picture. Move to the next phase."

The ambassador smoothed his hands down the front of his blue tunic and looked into the mirror on the wall. He carefully adjusted each golden button from the bottom up to the high neck of his shirt. When satisfied, he put his arms out and back to allow one of his staff to pull his dress robes into place. He shrugged to settle them comfortably before he brushed his hand over his head. The magic trailed from his palm and swirled through his long hair like a comb. It twisted the strands into a low ponytail and tied them securely. The energy dissipated upon completion and left his hair shimmering and fresh.

He smiled when he took a moment to appreciate the convenience of these little uses of magic. They made little demand on the battery he always carried tucked into a hidden pocket in his clothing. As one of the most advanced Mages, he no longer even had to consciously access the power and was also able to use his source efficiently. Besides, these small indulgences left time for more important matters, so it was miniscule energy well utilized to encourage greater benefit.

Satisfied, he walked over to the desk and slipped his feet into the blue satin loafers that matched his tunic and flowing blue pants. It was almost time for them to be on their way. The phone rang and he gestured to the staff, who immediately nodded and left the room. He answered the call. The video feature came up with the Federation Symbol instead of a face.

"Ambassador, this is Grant from the Federation security offices," the voice said.

V'ritan raised an eyebrow at the phone. "Yes? What do you need?"

The person cleared their throat nervously. "We called to tell you that your liaison didn't make it in time, but not to worry, we will have another sent out to you. They will be a few minutes late but will meet you at the event."

The ambassador stared at the screen for a moment and narrowed his eyes. He turned toward the mirror and read the trace of concern that had crept into his eyes. "No, never mind that. We will be fine for tonight. We will speak in the morning. Good evening."

Before the man could argue, the ambassador cut the call and stared at Brilgus.

"Sir, I have to insi…" *Click.* The ambassador hung up in the guy's ear.

He gritted his teeth and scowled as he flung the phone on the floor. "That pompous, arrogant asshole. How dare he hang up on me?"

Beta and the other team members entered the cheap motel room. The leader stared at him expectantly. "Well?"

The man shrugged. "He told me not to send anyone, that he would be fine for the night. Then he hung up on me before I could talk him into it. Jerk. He talks to anyone not Meligornian like they are dirt beneath his feet."

The ringleader had already pulled out another cigar and had it between his teeth. He bit on it, his expression sour. He patted the nervous man on the shoulder. "Don't worry about it. The hardest part is done. We don't have a gal on the inside but so what? We now know his state of mind going into tonight."

One of the other team members walked up, removed his coat, and draped it on the chair. "He didn't take the bait? To hell with it. That will be one less body to worry about tonight. It isn't a complete wash, so relax. We knew there would be a possibility he might flip our plans somewhat."

The man who had made the call leaned down and retrieved the phone, a pre-paid one from the gas station. He removed the battery, broke the device in two, and shrugged. "I suppose you're right. Every extra one of our men in there is a liability for the mission. Still, it irks me that he can be so nonchalant. Next time we need a government target, I say we pull that Booker guy. The senator who has had like three generations of family on the Senate. He seems like a pushover."

Beta raised his hands. "No more politics. Besides, we are only halfway done with this plan. The harder part is still ahead. We have to be prepared so get your damn minds straight. This isn't some amateur party. Don't make me look bad or I promise you, I will take you down with me."

———

Brilgus knocked quickly on the door and entered with the ambassador's thick outer robe in his arms. He laid it carefully across the chairs to avoid hair or wrinkles. V'ritan sat in his office chair and flipped through emails. He answered some and read and deleted others.

With his hands behind his back, the bodyguard cleared his throat. "Ambassador, if I may, I think that we need to talk about what is happening."

He sighed, closed out the email, and settled his attention on his companion with his hands folded at his waist. "Yes, dear friend and loyal businessman."

Brilgus stood tall and raised his chin in reverence but, at the same time, forcefulness. "It is absolutely necessary that we fix this before the event. You must have a liaison. They are vitally important to this event. I know you feel uneasy with the call you received, and I do not blame you. It sounds shady, to say the least, but we currently have men out to see if they can determine what went wrong."

V'ritan shook his head. "You may be right, but we don't have time to search and replace. And personally, I don't have the patience for it."

The bodyguard raised his hands and shook his head. "Dear Ambassador, had I known that was the issue, I would have offered my services long before now."

His employer raised both eyebrows. "And which service would that be today?"

Brilgus brandished his phone and smirked. "I happen to be very good at finding people in a pinch who can often be trusted more than the original ever could have been. I have, after all, worked for you for many years and we both know the young aides have a habit of running off or forgetting events. Don't worry about it. Relax, and I will make it happen. Would you like any tea?"

The ambassador shook his head. "Thank you, Brilgus. You have become an asset to this whole system."

CHAPTER TWENTY

S he hummed as she rubbed her hands through her soapy hair as the rainforest-like water showered over her. Sarah had put calming music on for her, but Stephanie was in the mood for something peppier that night. For the first time since the fight, she had excitement in her tone and step. The AI chose a dance music mix from the collection that Todd had created for her. They were all oldies, but it was her feel-good music.

There was something soothing about routine tasks that allowed her to do what she had to without having to focus too hard. She leaned her head back to wash the soap from her hair and smiled as the pressure from the water directly over her head increased. The suds shimmered in different colors as they floated around her feet and down the drain. When the soap was all out, Stephanie tapped her finger to her lips and leaned her head back again. "Lavender conditioner."

The spray of water stopped for a moment as conditioner pumped onto her hair. She smoothed it through and twisted her feet on the floor as she closed her eyes and jiggled her head in time to the beat. The fragrant perfume of the flowers eased into her lungs and a sense of calmness infused her. The water clicked on and she rinsed the conditioner out and turned the shower off with a verbal command.

Sarah spoke. "Your towel is on the wall. The shower drying will start as soon as you have exited. Are we going to blow dry?"

Stephanie shrugged. "Not tonight. I don't feel the vibe."

She wrapped one towel around her torso and flipped her head over to wrap a second one around her hair and tuck the end in at the base of her neck. She walked toward the door but paused for a moment. "Sarah, turn the music off."

The music clicked off and the sound of the phone ringing replaced it. Stephanie startled and hurried out. The door closed behind her and the quiet dryers began the process of drying the bathroom. She retrieved her tablet from the dresser and immediately saw the ambassador's number on the screen. Still in her towel, she thought about not answering but instead, responded in phone instead of video mode.

She shook her head and held the top of her towel closed. "Brilgus, so good to hear from you. I'm sorry I almost missed the call. I was showering."

"I was worried you were away from your phone," he said, and his voice sounded slightly panicked.

Stephanie backpedaled and sat on the edge of her chair. "Brilgus, what's the matter? You sound very upset."

"No, not upset," he replied. "But there always seems to be something going on. If it's not one thing it's another. As much as I like you and a few other full humans, I really do miss Meligorn."

Stephanie smiled understandingly. "I get that. There is really no place like home. No matter what state it's in. That's why I always understood why the Dreth who aren't pirates don't leave their planet, even with it in ruins. You work until all hope is gone, and only then do you give up on your home."

Brilgus chuckled. "You sure do sound cheerier today. I heard of your incident in DC. I'm sorry. I do hope your friend is recovering."

"He is," she replied. "He will be discharged tomorrow so it will be nice to welcome him back."

"Good. Give him my thanks for protecting you," the bodyguard replied. "But, now that I have exchanged pleasantries, and enjoyed them, I do have something to confess."

Stephanie giggled. "Don't we all, Brilgus. Okay, I'm ready for it. What do you have?"

"The ambassador needs a favor—and I suppose it's a favor for me as well," he said and winced through the words.

Meligornians were notorious for helping other people but never complained or asked for help in their own lives. But on Meligorn, there were rarely problems that weren't on a community scale. When the community knew, they would all come out, invited or not.

She looked at her wet hair in the mirror and realized vaguely that she needed a trim. "Sure, what do you need? Anything for you two."

Brilgus laughed. "I would reserve that until you've heard it. We need you to be the ambassador's liaison at a very important charity event this evening. We received a call that the regular person, for some reason, was unable to make it. The ambassador was not comfortable with how it was handled, so I thought you might be the perfect replacement."

Stephanie wrinkled her nose, having never attended an event like that. "All right. Tonight. Okay. When do I need to be there?"

Brilgus's nerves were almost audible. "An hour." Usually, the ambassador would meet with his liaison in his limo before the event and they would use the time to discuss things that might crop up while his personal security team conducted an additional sweep of the premises. This enabled them to establish what was expected but also allowed flexibility in his arrival to avoid traffic delays and to vary the direction and time of his approach to the venue. He'd been almost on his way when the call had come in, and both he and his bodyguard had accepted that this time, that buffer would have to be set aside.

Stephanie's eyes opened wide and she scowled at the closet. "Wow. Yikes. Okay, no need to panic. Of course I will do this. I must confess, though, I have neither been nor even heard of a liaison at these parties. What exactly do I have to do all night?"

"Ah, that is the easy part," Brilgus replied. "You simply remain at his side. He will spell his words to you so you hear them in English but to others, it will be Meligorn-speak. You will handle all communication with people until the ambassador takes over. This will include helping with appropriate customs between worlds and protection. Oh, there will be a security detail, so you needn't worry much about the protection part of things."

She pursed her lips. "And what worlds will be there?"

"It will be Earth and Meligorn, of course, and a couple of individuals from Dreth," he answered. "The Dreth know the customs well. It will mostly be the other humans whom you need to focus on. They don't always understand the greeting, the no touching, and what to say. I know you know most of it, and I will walk with the two of you so if you have any questions, you can simply ask me."

On one hand, the idea panicked her somewhat, but it also actually sounded like fun. "And what is the dress code for this occasion?"

Brilgus cleared his throat. "Formal. You may wear what is customary on Earth, the ambassador and I will be in our formal tunics and robes, and the Dreth...well, they have formal war gear so they will wear much the same as they usually do but with fewer blood stains."

Stephanie giggled. "At least they make an attempt. I personally pictured them like the Dreth pirates. I've never met a Dreth before. Well, one, but it was very brief."

The bodyguard snarled slightly with evident distaste. "Yes, they are interesting. Although these two are generally more well-mannered than the citizens there. They are part of the royal chamber on their planet, so they have been given some instruction. They don't have a formal greeting, so you only need to worry about their greeting to the ambassador. He is usually fairly open-minded about them, regardless whether they actually perform it right or not at all. Most likely, though, they will miss the greetings as usual and end the evening with a goodbye instead."

Stephanie exhaled a deep breath. "All right, that sounds good. Where do I go?"

Brilgus mumbled to himself a moment. "Ah, that's right. It is the Grand Legion of Federation Fine Arts located where the Old Days Lincoln Memorial stood once. We will have you on the list."

Stephanie jotted that down on the virtual notepad function on her tablet. "Good. Right, then. That should be easy to find, then. But to make it on time, I need to go. When I arrive, I will send you a text and wait on the steps for you."

"That sounds perfect," he replied. "And thank you, Stephanie. This means a lot."

She hung up, looked around her in bemusement for a moment, and bounded to her feet in a panic. "Sarah! I need the black and silver butterfly formal gown and several shoe selections including something practical in case any running or fighting is involved. And my *hairrr!*"

Sarah began to take the appropriate measures. "It would be good if you were to calm down. You are starting to panic and that increases heart rate, confusion, and the chance of a stroke."

Stephanie stuck her head out the bathroom door to yell above the blow dryer. "I'll stroke anyway if we don't get this right."

A bell chimed and the hair dryer stopped. Stephanie scrambled into her bra and panties and peered cautiously at the comms video screen. It was Elizabeth so she clicked the button and smiled. "Hey, what's up?"

The other woman raised an eyebrow. "Are you all right? It

suddenly sounded as if a herd of buffalo rampaged through your room. Are you having a fit? I can tranquilize you with one of the darts from the dart gun."

Stephanie gave her a deadpan stare. "No. I just had a call from the ambassador, and he needs me to be his liaison tonight at a charity event. Something happened to his. So, I have less than an hour to get ready and get over there. Not to mention that I've never been one before."

Elizabeth's face remained expressionless. "I know. Sarah has already filled me in, which is really why I called. I want to send Lars and Marcus with you as backup. The security will be Federation Secret Service who are trained like offbeat cops, and none of them are too bright."

She shrugged. "All right. I'm sure it won't be a problem. The ambassador understands that I am not a person who gallivants around on my own anymore so he should expect that I would have my own security. There is one problem, though."

Elizabeth raised her eyebrows. "Yes?"

Stephanie chewed the inside of her lip. "They need to have tickets to the event. You can't simply buy the tickets as they are invite only, of course. Brilgus put me on but not anyone with me."

"Have you forgotten who you are talking to here? I am the woman who literally spent years in a job where my only task was to retrieve anything that they needed. My own personal brand of magic has its own power in that world. I once had to retrieve a small lamp like the one in that Aladdin story that was specifically last seen in the chamber room of the queen's area in the pyramids in Egypt. That was interesting, and the best part? Thirty-six hours later, I had it polished, sitting on a pillow, and in my lap traveling back. I wanted to rub it so badly."

Stephanie giggled and then jumped. "So, you'll handle the tickets and make sure they are appropriately dressed?"

She winked cheerfully. "I've got you, sister."

Elizabeth's red-painted lips smirked as she picked up the phone and dialed the guard's quarters. Marcus answered. "Oh, good, I needed to speak to you and Lars. Where is he?"

"Right here," the man yelled. They obviously had her on speaker phone.

Her lip twitched slightly. "I need the two of you to get your tuxes out, dust them off, shine your shoes, conceal your weapons, and be ready in forty-five. You will accompany Stephanie to a charity event where she will be the acting liaison to the Head Ambassador of Meligorn."

Marcus wasn't sure what to say. "Uh…uh… Okay…I…"

Elizabeth rolled her eyes. "Oh, for Christ's sake, get it together man. Lars, get on it."

"On it," he yelled from the back before the call disconnected.

She shook her head and ambled across the room to retrieve her tablet and open a video chat. Once she sat comfortably, she flipped to the number to connect her to the boss, leaned back, and crossed her legs. When he answered, the hologram of the company spiraled around in midair as usual.

"I thought you would be asleep or torturing someone by now," BURT said in greeting, having adjusted his sarcasm level the day before.

Elizabeth furrowed her brow. "You are mighty feisty tonight. Do you have a hot date or something?"

BURT paused. "Oh yeah, me and my server will go on a whirlwind adventure across Meligorn."

She yawned. "Mm-hmm. Sounds lovely. But I need you to do something for me really fast before you ship off to Never-Never Land with some AI. And I don't need the details. There are plenty of men out there with computer girlfriends, but I didn't peg you as one."

"What would you peg me as, then?" he asked.

Elizabeth raised both eyebrows and pursed her lips. "Honestly? Gay, actually."

BURT queried this but stopped hurriedly. "I see. No, though I think I fall more into the asexual category. Anyway, what can I do for you?"

She leaned forward. "I need you to get Lars and Marcus tickets to the Grand Legion of Federation Fine Arts Charity Ball tonight. Stephanie has been asked to act as the liaison for the ambassador and I want two of our men there to protect her."

He immediately sifted through the system and hacked into their guest list database. Elizabeth wasn't sure what he was doing but gave him time to respond since he was more than a little strange. A few moments later, he was done. "All right, they are on the list. I have pull almost everywhere for tickets."

Her mouth dropped slightly. "Oh. Right…okay. Thanks, then."

BURT definitely had pull, but it just so happened to be the kind that required him to hack into a highly classified system without being traced or caught. Luckily, he was a much more intelligent system than any of their other Federation protocols, so it was like taking candy from a baby.

Elizabeth hung up and stood when she heard someone walk down the hall. She yanked the door open so quickly she actually scared Stephanie. Elizabeth looked at the girl for a moment, taken aback. She wore a strapless black velvet dress that was tight in the bodice to her waist, where it flared out and came to her calves. Underneath were rows and rows of black and silver crinoline and artfully arranged from the bottom up to about halfway were silver glittering butterflies in a garden of lilies. One of the lilies' stems curved from the side along the bottom of her breasts and up to the right side of her bodice. It was an amazing gown.

Stephanie's hair and makeup were incredible too. Her hair was pulled back into a tight, smooth, perfect bun at the nape of her neck. What looked like thin silver vines wound around it.

Her eyes were very dramatic and almost resembled the black and silver wings of the butterflies on the dress, and her lips were a deep rose.

Elizabeth shook her head. "You look absolutely amazing. Really, so gorgeous. I knew you were a pretty girl, but this is model... *Oh, my God.* What are those *hideously practical shoes?*"

The girl looked at the offending shoes—a pair of black slip-ons but with the rubber non-slip soles and slightly chunky bottoms. She shrugged. "I need practical in case anything happens."

The other woman sneered in genuine horror. "You couldn't have strappy silver heels and go barefoot if anything happened?"

Stephanie narrowed her eyes. "Have you seen the streets out there? It's like dipping your body in tetanus. I like life right now."

Elizabeth sighed. "Good point, but good God."

CHAPTER TWENTY-ONE

The car pulled up at the event and the two guards exited first. Lars stood at the door and extended his hand to help her from the car. He whispered through his smile. "Not that you need my help in those frighteningly practical shoes from the back storage room of some rundown steakhouse waitress in Louisiana."

Stephanie snatched her hand away and turned to smile kindly at the people who passed them. She slammed her practically-shod foot down on Lars's instep and he hissed and tried to keep his composure. "Oh, look, the ambassador just arrived."

She moved down the steps and waited as Brilgus climbed out, looked at her, and smiled widely. He mouthed, "Wow," pointed at her dress, and stepped aside. The ambassador emerged and waved and smiled at the press as they snapped pictures as fast as they could. The droid reporters hovered overhead and tried to hear quiet conversations, but most of the Meligornian delegates would have a mild charm active to shield their discussions. These used little energy and spilled over those in close proximity, so in practical terms, the event itself had been charmed to ensure a degree of secrecy.

As they started up the steps, the ambassador studied Stephanie approvingly and extended his arm to her. She walked beside him, her arm wound around his. "You look very beautiful. And I am glad you brought a couple of your men. If they are of sufficient caliber to protect you, I would trust them with my life."

Stephanie chuckled. "They don't let me go out unsupervised. But it's a good thing."

V'ritan winked. "They don't let me go out unsupervised either. Welcome to the world of being treated like precious cargo. It will be annoying."

"Ten minutes before it ever happened? Yep, I'm there. But they are my family now and they put themselves on the line for me so I will smile the whole time."

The ambassador stopped at the door. "Good. Are you ready for this? I'm already over it."

Beta walked through the doors of the Fine Arts Ball. Carefully applied makeup covered the scars on his face, and contacts changed the color of his eyes to blue. His dark hair was slicked back, and his tux was perfectly pressed and worth more money than most people in the subs made in two years. He sauntered through the security check, handed them his silver cane, and allowed them to inspect it before he continued.

At the bar, he ordered a scotch, turned casually, and scrutinized the sea of people who entered for the night's festivities. A voice spoke quietly in his ear. "We are all in position."

Beta's gaze shifted lazily to each of the places checked on the blueprints that they had worked with. He smiled inwardly as he confirmed that each of his men had taken their position, all strategically located around the perimeter of the building. They were dressed to the hilt and had been told to focus on the art to look non-threatening, and to keep their specially equipped vests completely out of view. Not only were they bulletproof, but they stored all their guns and were completely undetectable by the security metal checks.

He carried two pistols in the vest, one laser and one regular ammo although he still hadn't fully caught on to the laser fad. Satisfied that all had proceeded according to plan, he turned and pretended to yawn, then completed the movement of his hand to unobtrusively brush his finger on his earpiece. "This is where you will stay until I give the word. Remember, if it looks or feels too suspicious to stand in the same spot, call for a rotation and you will all move up one spot. We didn't get this far to be nabbed by Federation blue-coats."

"Roger that," each of them said into their comms.

Beta turned to study the crowd once more. Slowly, a smirk stretched his lips and he chuckled. He felt that he still had it. Even after all those years of having a seat at the table and sending errand boys to do the dirty work, he was still exceptional at what he did. It had been a very long time for him, but when everything went as planned that night, he would be handsomely rewarded and possibly named as the next Full Leader when the position became available.

A woman in a long, red, sequined, backless dress walked past him with a glimmer in her eye. She licked her top lip, but Beta simply stared at her and blinked. Without any return affection, she walked awkwardly away. He pursed his lips and shook his head. "Damn human women. They have no idea."

"I wish that when we came to these shindigs, we could wear tuxes instead of our navy dress formals," Vice Admiral Blanton whispered as he ascended the steps.

Admiral Suffix chuckled. "Trust me, I totally understand. They have updated all the Federation Navy uniforms to fit with the times, but when it came to these, they decided to go with a George and Martha Washington time period. They even took away the long dress pants and gave us these abominable things. I cannot believe I had to ask for a pair of...pantaloons—formal pantaloons. I am a grown-ass man."

Blanton snickered. "A grown-ass man who could also wear a white wig, a pair of round glasses, and fly a kite into a storm to discover electricity."

The other man covered his mouth and laughed but ended with a cough to disguise it. "What was that revamp of an Old Broadway play they sent us to last year?"

Blanton snapped his fingers. "Oh...uh...*Newsies*."

"That's it. You're Jack "Cowboy" Kelly and I'm Bryan Denton."

The men laughed all the way up the stairs and into the building. The lead security waved them away from the metal detectors. "Admiral Suffix, Vice Admiral Blanton, it's so good that you are here. I wanted to escort you through this maze since you are the only guests in attendance permitted to keep your weapons on your person. All except, of course, the secret service."

The admiral nodded. "We appreciate it. Although I haven't quite figured out why it is a mandatory part of the formal attire yet."

Vice Admiral Blanton shrugged. "You know us crazy navy folk. We go riding into full-on battles in our formals all the time."

All three chuckled and the agent opened the gate to allow them through. "Have a good evening, gentlemen."

They entered and paused to look around at the people. Suffix sneered. "And we are expected to speak to all of them." He sighed dramatically. "If I'd known as a new recruit that this was what they meant when they talked about making sacrifices for the nation..."

. . .

His companion laughed. "We're window-dressing, Admiral. Part of the politics of the position. It does, however, afford us a rare opportunity to hear things that might otherwise not be said. People tend to relax at these events. It's not so much that we need to talk to them, but that we need to listen." He shuddered. "It's a pity, though, that we have to listen to all the bull-crap too."

They stood there silently for a moment, focused on the giddy faces, fancy clothes, and important figures. Finally, Blanton put his hand on the admiral's shoulder and leaned in. "Shall we get a drink?"

Suffix took a deep breath and tugged on his pantaloons. "I think that's a hell of an idea. I knew I was friends with you for a reason."

Blanton chuckled. "You mean besides the fact that I'm the only one close enough to your rank to allow a friendship?"

The admiral smacked his lips and his gray mustache rose and fell. "Hmm. Yes. That too. Although I could have gotten worse. Old Admiral Phillips with his broken hips and wrinkled old body could still be here."

They walked toward the bar. Blanton smirked. "He did have a nice monocle."

***

The music from inside the gala could be heard all across the Mall and down through the abandoned streets and old government buildings. The venue was lit up brighter than daylight with sparkling holographic golden stars that shimmered down the façade like falling magic snow. From both corners of the building, large spotlights were turned on and streamed the images of the Federation symbol, the NorAm's Stars and Stripes, Meligorn's Pantigordia flower, the symbol of peace in the country, and the slightly harsher helmet and warrior glove of Dreth.

The news vans were set up all along the press line. Some

already rolled footage of the event while others set up for the evening's light show and celebrity appearances. The event had become what awards shows had been in the old days. The whole world watched to catch a glimpse of the most glamorous, most chivalrous, and most famous people in the Federation. The money raised was merely a plus, an endowment set up for children of the fallen Federation sailors and soldiers. Of course, it usually was panhandled in bribes barely days later but the idea of it let the richies feel good about donating to the little orphaned urchins on the streets.

It was, in reality, merely another manifestation of the class structure and made the poor seem even poorer and the middle class work harder toward a higher level. Class structure in the United States forever grew farther apart. But that was not even close to the biggest worries that the Federation would soon face and were willfully ignorant of.

CHAPTER TWENTY-TWO

Beta moved casually across the room and observed the ambassador keenly from afar. He had to admit, the man was very powerful, very well-liked, and very intelligent. He knew, even though the humans refused to admit it, that Meligornians, even the lowliest, had IQs past genius level on Earth. It wasn't due to anything other than a species difference. But, of course, the pride of the human species kept them from celebrating it. Denial was something all humans seemed to be good at. They denied crimes, infidelities, rule-breaking, and even facts. They would get so caught up in the lies that even when presented with the cold, hard facts, they would deny that they were real.

This was a very good reason why the Federation still controlled everyone, despite the frequent uprisings and battles through their history. The government always maintained control. Meligorn was truly free, understanding of faults, and knowledgeable of coercion but never practiced it. They were truly the better species, but they were also hated by the Dreth and many of the richie humans as well.

One of Beta's men spoke over the comms. "It looks like the ambassador brought his own liaison."

Another man chuckled. "Yes. He. Did. And I have to say she is hot as hell—except for those shoes… I don't understand."

Beta's gaze dipped to the shoes rather than the wearer. "They seem practical." He had no interest in the woman. Liaisons were expendable and whoever this was would pose no problems. Her presence there was probably more a PR exercise than anything else. He was more concerned with identifying the security detail that would inevitably have infiltrated the crowd.

The first man laughed. "It sucks to be her tonight. She should have called in sick. Those little fateful decisions you make and never think they will be your last. So sad. A waste of a beautiful face."

One of others coughed in the comm. "Ahem. Ass…oh, sorry, I have this cough."

Beta clenched his jaw and looked down to hide his irritation as he growled into the comms. "Could we stop acting like this is Fashion Runway or The Female Auctions? We are here to do a job. Thereafter, what you talk about is none of my business."

Everyone fell silent and kept their eyes on the prize—the end of the ambassador and the line of bullshit they so avidly hated.

V'ritan walked between Brilgus and Stephanie, his hands locked together inside his long robe sleeves and a pleasant smile on his face. The bodyguard stood tall, his chest puffed out, and his eyes continually scanned the immediate crowd around them. On either side, four secret service agents, stoic and alert, studied the people and the surroundings in search of any sign of trouble. Last but not least, Marcus and Lars fell in behind as a rearguard and continually turned to sweep the room behind them.

As for Stephanie, she was beyond amazing at the job. She had a bright and kind smile and she found that when she was forced into a position where she needed to be likable, she was actually able to be open and warm with people. They reacted well to her and she handled a number of small meetings very efficiently and without mistakes. But every party of a political nature always came with an asshole.

She stood beside V'ritan with a welcoming smile and sparkling eyes and waited for the next guest. A small prickle of warning made her look up at a middle-aged man with a horse-shoe bald spot and a very round middle. He seemed obviously intoxicated and stumbled toward them with his finger pointed.

Stephanie immediately became defensive and stepped in front of him so he couldn't reach the ambassador. He stared dismissively at her. "Who are you? Some NorAm ho to keep him happy while he's here?"

Brilgus tightened his fist and the ambassador glanced at him and shook his head. Stephanie summoned a huge fake smile and pushed her fingers into the man's chest. "Why have you come to speak to the ambassador today?"

He laughed. "To tell him I know he's full of shit. I know his people are full of shit. They are trying to take us over and the Federation, run by a bunch of pansies, can't stop sucking on the Meligorn teat long enough to see it. I want him to know I see it. And that I don't understand because we've been so nice to them."

She glanced at the secret service agents and shook her head before she drew the man's jacket closed and patted him hard on the chest. "I'm going to say something to you right now and I want you to know it is in your very best interest. And when you are sober, you will think about this and thank me for it."

He frowned and his head wobbled slightly. "What?"

Stephanie sucked in a deep breath through her mouth and continued. "You are making an ass of yourself. And that means you are making an ass out of everyone on Earth. Believe it or not, we are all representatives of this planet. Now, I want you to go back to the restroom, wash the idiot out of your mouth, and try to come back with at least a modicum of respect and class. If you do that, I might be able to help you. I know you have class some-where, because only those who hold the dollar hold the tickets to the golden palace. So go and find some."

The two security guards on either side both immediately lowered their heads and pressed their lips together. They tried desperately not to laugh as the guy looked at her in confusion before he stumbled off. She glanced at them and shook her head. They were young secret service, but not as dense as she had expected. In fact, they seemed to really take their jobs seriously, which was good since they were protecting the most important Meligornian political figure on Earth.

"Here's the glass of seltzer you wanted," the reporter's assistant said, slightly out of breath from climbing all the way up into the high levels.

She took the water and grabbed a napkin to blot a wine stain on the hem of her dress. "Stupid drunk richies. They don't give a damn about anyone. I honestly want to get this footage and get the hell out of here already."

The reporter stood, grabbed the camera, and walked to the edge. She tilted it forward and scanned the crowds to record footage of the events below. It didn't help her mood that her usual cameraman had dropped the assignment in favor of greener pastures. She hated camerawork although she wasn't half bad at it, but this gig might well be her ticket to the big-time. If she could snag some decent and more intimate footage than the drones and commercial stations, she might slide a foot in the right door.

She set the camera on the stand and her assistant made sure she was in focus. Behind her, silent holographic fireworks burst to create a ceiling of sparkling joy for the richies—and an annoying hindrance of footage for her.

The assistant nodded and counted down with his fingers, then pointed to the reporter who now held her mic in hand.

Cindy and Mark picked their sandwiches up from the counter and wandered over to slide into one of the booths. She exhaled a deep breath and shook her head. "This building is amazing but I can't wait to hire more people so we don't have to do this constantly."

Mark nodded and took a big bite of his sandwich. "At least we get a break."

She snapped her fingers and pointed at him. "You are the king of glass half full. This is why I love you."

He pumped his fist. "Boy meets girl, boy courts girl, girl is repulsed, boy gives daily motivational quotes and pep talks, girl finally loves boy."

Cindy giggled and glanced up as the deli man turned the news on. "This is Veada Bowls with Federation Entertainment News coming to you live from the Federation Arts Gala and Charity Event. As you know, this is the biggest event of the season, bringing in celebrities, political heads, and the most influential people of this decade."

She ate her sandwich, thoroughly exhausted, and simply stared at the footage on the screen. Suddenly, her head jerked, and she choked, covering her full mouth. Mark looked at her and she pointed wildly at the screen. When he turned, his wide eyes matched hers as they watched their daughter lead the Ambassador of Meligorn around one of the most prestigious events in the world.

Cindy gave a maternal sigh and tilted her head to the side. "Oh, she looks so beautiful. She is knocking them dead."

Brilgus leaned over and whispered to Stephanie. "You had better watch out or he might try to bring you on full time."

She rolled her eyes. "Over my dead body."

Gunfire blazed ahead of them and screams rang out. Brilgus put his body in front of the ambassador and Stephanie whipped her head around to see where it came from. She turned instinctively to the Secret Service agent on her left. Before she could call to him, his head snapped back, and blood splattered on the ground behind him as his body fell heavily. She ducked and spun to the other agent on her right. He had his gun up and fired into the open levels above and ahead of them.

Suddenly, his body jerked to the right, then to the left, and finally landed hard on the steps. He groaned, raised his weapon, and fired. A man screamed and his body went limp as he toppled over the balcony and plummeted to the floor below. The agent slid his gun over a smidge and pulled the trigger. It sounded like a cannon as both the sharpshooter and the agent fired at the same time. A bullet slammed into the agent's forehead to finish him off. At the same time, the other sharpshooter tumbled over the balcony and fell to his death below.

Brilgus, his arms shielding the ambassador, walked his employer toward the back of the venue. Another barrage of shots erupted to strike the ceiling and spray chunks of plaster onto the crowd. Everyone crouched and scanned the room frantically to find some kind of cover. Seven men pushed out of the crowds, distinguishable from the other guests only by the weapons they now trained on the ambassadorial group.

Beta walked forward, a toothpick in the corner of his mouth and a glass of scotch in his hand. Lars and Marcus shoved through the crowd and hurried to the middle of the grand staircase where Stephanie and everyone else now stood.

He flipped his toothpick to the other cheek and looked at his drink before he yelled, "I know, this is supposed to be a party, huh? Yeah, everyone hates a party crasher. Let's be honest with each other here, sweet little girl."

The man studied the so-called sweet little girl with a sudden sense of unease. Something within him said he should recognize this woman—she was certainly the type to be readily remembered—yet he couldn't quite place her. His gaze swept rapidly over her and triggered a response. She reminded him a little of the witch, he realized, and grinned. There was no way that scruffy teenage magical-wanna-be could even begin to compare. Satisfied that he'd traced the odd sense of familiarity, he turned his attention back to the matter in hand.

"We appreciate heroic actions here and everything but there are three of you—only two armed—and seven of us. I feel like a smart person would put their guns down and walk away. So I'll give you that option. You get your buddies to throw them down, and the three of you can walk out. And you won't even have messed up your dress. What do you say?"

Stephanie snickered and Lars shook his head. She set her clutch on the ground with a slow, deliberate movement, tugged at the black satin wrist gloves she wore, and slowly inched a hand down the front of her dress. Beta pursed his lips as his gaze followed the almost sensual gesture. His eyes widened when she drew a compact long-barrel pistol from between her breasts and pointed it at his head. Brilgus had slipped it to her with a grin and a wink a few minutes after their arrival, and she'd been delighted that it had nestled so snugly in the cushioned holster Mother Nature had provided.

Everyone was silent for a moment and Stephanie leaned forward. "How dare you come into this party, among my friends and my people, and think that you can take lives without repercussions? And don't you ever stand there and tell me the odds when the other team is chock-full of assholes!"

She gestured dismissively and nodded with a smirk. "Oh, and my dress? It's stain resistant."

Lars and Marcus immediately opened fire and the trio raced across the staircase and slid to dodge a volley of return fire. Stephanie aimed at Beta and he smiled as he backed slowly out of sight and headed for the front doors. He didn't intend to stick around for this.

Suddenly, the ambassador used his magic to push Brilgus aside. He flung his arms back to throw his robes off and onto the ground. His expression grim, he summoned his energy and launched into a concerted attack. Death balls of magic spiraled at the assassins in a relentless barrage. He hurried forward and stood beside Stephanie, glanced quickly at her, and winked when he eliminated three of the men, whose bodies instantly ignited with magical fire.

It was a trick Stephanie hadn't seen before, but she loved it. They felt as if they were burning alive in torturous agony, but when the magic dissipated, there wouldn't be a scratch on anything but their pride. She shot her last bullet and fumbled under her dress to retrieve another mag and thrust it in place. She raised it, ready to fire, when Lars flailed back with blood flooding down his arm and over his hand. He smacked into the steps and groaned.

"*Nooo*," Stephanie screamed.

She clenched her jaw and descended slowly, one step at a time, firing relentlessly at one of the assassins at the base of the stairs. Her slugs connected with his flack vest twice before she adjusted her aim. His eyes widened as her gun focused on his head. She pulled the trigger and his body catapulted away and landed to slide across the marble floor. Two more secret service agents went down, one to the far right of her and another in the main venue who tried to reach the gunmen.

At that point, everything seemed to move in slow motion. She backed up the steps again and paused beside the ambassador. He stared at her, his gaze fixed, his mouth slightly open, and his brow creased. She knew immediately that something was wrong, and her gaze fell to his stomach where he gripped it tightly with one hand. Blood seeped between his fingers.

Stephanie grabbed him by the shoulders as he fell and eased him down. She breathed heavily and scowled at the wound, uncertain that he could survive it. Desperately, she pushed to her feet and tried to find Brilgus. As she stepped forward, a shot rang out and the bullet struck home in her right shoulder blade. She tumbled forward and her gaze found Marcus. Blood streamed from his thigh, and beyond him, Brilgus continued to shoot despite a painful flesh wound on his huge arm.

She landed hard and her head sagged. Her gaze settled on the ambassador's face. His eyes focused on her and although he didn't open his mouth, she swore she could hear him speak. *You have the power, Morgana. You know what to do. Your fear is the only thing holding you back.*

Stephanie gritted her teeth and forced herself into a sitting position. She fumbled for her purse and suppressed the instinctive scream at the pain that seared in her shoulder. Her hands weak and trembling, she managed to retrieve the battery from her bag and gripped it tightly in her hand. For a moment, she felt the energy of Meligorn, but something else began to tingle and pulse through that magic, calling for her.

Her arm dropped and her hand released the battery. She closed her eyes and pushed past the pain to focus only on the sounds of the energy around her. On instinct, she focused her mind on the Earth's ley lines to draw the energy and magic of humans into her body. Like a warm, welcome presence, a slow wave of energy seeped into every part of her.

Everything but the awareness of the power faded. While on one level, she was aware of her injury and even of the excruciating pain, she seemed to have somehow stepped beyond it to a place where she functioned on the energy alone. She opened her eyes.

Her pupils had once again become dark black and her mind

was suddenly able to distinguish each distinct crack as a weapon fired. She first identified a man on the balcony level above them and all the way to the right. The energy pulsed within her as she snapped her head toward him and extended her arm with her palm up and her hand curled into a claw-like shape. She flung the magic and directed it to grip the ceiling above him and rip it down piecemeal. In moments, it had showered him with huge marble stones until the only thing left to see was his limp hand that hung lifelessly between the railings.

She slid her focus to an assassin standing front and center—the one who had wounded the ambassador and most likely shot her friends as well. Anger blew through her and she screamed, the sound of something otherworldly that echoed violently from her chest. She clenched her fist tightly and hauled her arm back. The man wheezed and clutched his neck as his body rose and levitated toward her. He stopped inches away, his eyes wide as he choked on the invisible force. She turned to the side and kicked hard to pound her foot into his crotch. The magic released him, and he fell to curl into a fetal position and writhe in pain.

Stephanie spat at him before she swished both arms to the right and swiftly to the left. The man's body careened over the heads of the cowering richies and crashed through the plate-glass window and out onto the lawn. Shots rang out again, but not at her. The attackers continued to shoot at her people. She jerked her fists upward and slammed them down hard on the marble steps. The energy rocketed out, splitting the stone, and rose into a high barrier. It wavered there as a bright blue shimmering haze. The bullets bounced off and ricocheted back at the gunmen.

She thrust her hand through the protective shield, gripped the air, and twisted hard. A man panicked when he lost control of his own hand. It turned toward him, his finger on the trigger. He shoved the barrel to his forehead and screamed until the shot echoed and his shriek fell silent.

CHAPTER TWENTY-THREE

Stephanie withdrew her hand through the barrier and walked slowly toward the ambassador. As she approached, the crack of gunfire distracted her once more. She whipped around and immediately created a hole in her shield to walk through. Her eyes angry, she stopped and stared at the floor below. The guests had created a battle arena when they ran and cowered against the sides of the room.

Two gunmen lay dead on the ground and blood pooled around them. Standing behind them, their guns out, stood the admiral and vice admiral. The two additional assassins had tried to sneak in, but the officers had noticed them and were able to intercept and eliminate the threat. Stephanie nodded her head at the naval dignitaries, and they returned the gesture. She turned away and hurried over to V'ritan. As she dropped to her knees beside him, Brilgus walked toward them and shook his head in disbelief.

The ambassador took her hand and tugged it to hover over where the wound was. She stared into his eyes for several moments before she focused on the bloody, gaping hole. He opened his mouth to speak but she shook her head and closed her eyes. She centered herself and drew back from the frenzy of the battle. Her energy pushed down into the palm of her hand and light began to permeate from her palm. The Meligornian magic inside the ambassador—the little he had left—spiraled from the wound, attracted by her energy.

The two trails of magic hovered mere centimeters apart for several moments. Grunting with effort, Stephanie pushed harder, and the energy connected to release a wave of light. Wind whipped wildly around the two of them and Stephanie's arm shook so violently that she had to use her other to stabilize it. Everyone around them backed away as the force of the magic merging created almost a force field around them. Slowly, the tendrils of Meligornian magic drew the light magic down into the ambassador's body. He groaned and his head tilted back as the energy surged through him and out of Stephanie.

Even with her eyes closed, she could see the ambassador. She could see him in the fields of Meligorn in youth and in his early years of marriage. He danced with a beautiful little girl and she could hear the child's laughter echo around them. A surge of pain —not physical, but emotional—pounded into her chest and almost knocked her back. She struggled to hold her hand firm and watched as he stood in that field where they'd danced, surrounded by so many Meligornian men and women. He clung tightly to his wife and they watched as sparkling and shimmering specs of their daughter's soul rose from her flower-shrouded body up toward the heavens, through the MU spectrum, and out into the stars.

Stephanie gasped and her chest pushed forward, and her shoulders thrust back as more and more visions of him hurtled through her mind like a homemade movie. So much sadness and pain, so much loss. What she thought she knew before all seemed so simple compared to the truth that dangled over her as her magic healed his. After several more intense moments, the two energies separated. She fell back on the stairs and her body ached all over. After a long moment, she opened her eyes and shook off the flooded field of emotion that slithered through her down to her soul. Her energy was severely drained, but she wasn't done. There were so many who needed healing.

Brilgus hurried down the steps now that the energy had dissipated and knelt beside the ambassador. Slowly, the Meligornian opened his eyes and blinked a couple of times before he sat up. His energy had been restored and the dried blood on his clothes and skin were the only remnants of the wound. He turned quickly in search of Stephanie. She nodded at him and their eyes connected for a moment. He knew what she had seen, and she knew it was not for her to speak of. It was an unfortunate reaction to the healing powers that they had combined, but it was private.

V'ritan put his hand up and allowed Brilgus to help him to his feet. He felt better than he had in years, like he had lost a hundred years from his life. He walked over and lifted Stephanie by her shoulders. She paused and furrowed her brow. "It doesn't hurt anymore."

Startled, she looked over her shoulder to find nothing more than dried blood and no wound. The ambassador smiled. "We healed each other. Now, let's heal the rest of them, shall we?"

Stephanie nodded, turned, and knelt beside Lars. He looked at her and groaned. "I thought this was only a party. Who gets shot at a party in the richie neighborhood?"

She chuckled and held her hand over his shoulder to allow her energy to pulsate through his wound. He hissed in pain, but she maintained the pressure and pushed the magic into him until it stopped of its own accord. She moved her hand and smiled when she confirmed that the wound was gone. Lars was in shock and awe, completely speechless for once in his life. His eyes drifted over her and he jumped up. "Marcus!"

The other man grumbled and gripped his thigh tightly. "This

is the worst. I'll take your punishment. These white people went super ghetto in here. This is bullshit."

Stephanie laughed and sat beside him to put her hands on his leg. He grimaced and scrunched his face for several moments until finally, he began to relax. The energy seeped into his wounds to heal him from the inside out. When it disconnected, she raised her hand, satisfied with her work. Marcus poked at it and looked in shock for a moment before he grabbed her by the arms and yanked her into a tight hug. "You are a shit-hot witch, you know that? You don't play. Thank you."

He pulled back and looked keenly at her, seeing the tiredness that had settled over her face. "Hey, you should give it a break. The ambassador has got it."

Stephanie rubbed her face and shook her head. "No. I gotta do this."

She stood and shuffled to the first victim she could find, a Federation guard with a bullet wound to the bicep. He watched her with tears in his eyes as she wrapped her hands around his arm and closed her eyes. It was strange to her. She had gone her whole life without that much Earth energy inside her but once she'd experienced it, when it began to wane, it felt almost painful. Like the life was sucked from her chest. But she had to help these people. They had put their lives on the line to help her and she couldn't let them suffer on the steps while the very people they hated for their ignorance and money stared at them from the perimeter.

As the magic disconnected from the healed wound, Stephanie fell back and grasped instinctively for something solid to hold onto. Lars hurried behind her and steadied her. She had given everything she had to give and then some. The ambassador had taken care of the other wounded, and Brilgus carefully carried the fallen guards' bodies to the marbled platform halfway down the steps.

Stephanie looked at Lars. "Help me down there."

He nodded, picked her up, and cradled her in his arms. He walked down and held her as she watched the ambassador whisper in Meligornian and sprinkle magical energy over their bodies, extending the ultimate respect to their fallen souls. They had been the only protection between him and death, and he owed them more than that, but it was the best he could do. The entire place had fallen completely silent and the Meligornian song drifted quietly through it like a whisper in a wind. Every person whose ears it touched began to feel a lightness in their soul. The fear began to dissipate, and the tears started to dry.

Marcus gasped as he stared beyond Lars and Stephanie and down at the entryway below. Standing, all in ranks and saluting, was the Federation Navy. They had arrived too late to help, but not too late to pay tribute to the bodies strewn around the floors. Brilgus came back down the steps and put his hand on the ambassador's shoulder. "We have to go."

The bodyguard looked at Lars, Stephanie, and Marcus. "All of us. We need to leave before the media breaks into a frenzy. Meligornians do not speak to the media after such a tragic incident. I have a car waiting out back, but we need to go now."

Lars carried her the entire way as Brilgus hurried them through the great dining hall and out the back exit. A car waited, the doors already open for them. The ambassador got in the back first and everyone followed until the bodyguard scooted in and shut the door. The windows were all darkly tinted and a partition separated the front and the back. Stephanie lay in Lars's lap, everything fuzzy and foggy.

Brilgus motioned quickly and the entire roof shimmered into translucence to reveal the stars high up in the sky. Stephanie turned her head to stare upward. The night sky consumed her and the moon, so crisp and bright, stared back. A tear collected at the outward edge of her eye and trickled down her cheek. She could hear everyone talking, but it was so muffled like it was a million miles away. As her eyes locked on the rarely present

Milky Way, her body gave in to the exhaustion. Her eyes closed and the sounds ceased as she drifted into a deep, all-consuming sleep.

With her eyes still clenched shut, Stephanie swallowed and grimaced at how dry everything was. She licked her lips and tasted something sweet that she couldn't identify. It took more effort than it should to roll onto her stomach and she ran her hands along the soft sheets below her. As nice as it was, she immediately realized it was not anywhere she had ever been before. Immediately, her eyes blinked open and she turned over and hauled the gossamer blankets up to her chin.

The room was oddly familiar, a smaller, more decorated version of the temple on Meligorn. She scooted to a sitting position and looked around her. If she had never known about Meligorn, she would have sworn she was in the castle bedroom of some medieval princess. But no, she was in a Meligornian bedroom. She could see the beautiful purple haze and the bright illumination shining through the paneled window on two walls of the room.

The light cascaded through the panes of glass and over the stone floor. Beautiful, plush draperies hung from not only the windows but the walls as well. Fresh flowers sat in multiple vases throughout the space, and the sweetness, she realized, was not on her lips but in her nose. It was the sweetness of the room she could almost taste.

She pulled her knees to her chest and smiled, uncertain as to whether she was actually in a dream or not. Either way, it was absolutely amazing and so entrancing that she barely heard the creak of the doorknob. As she turned to look, the handle turned, paused, and the door began to open.

CHAPTER TWENTY-FOUR

She actually held her breath when the door creaked on its hinges as it opened slowly. Stephanie put her fists down on the bed beside her, too weary to react. The last thing she remembered was the stars floating gently overhead as they drove away from the grizzly scene that had unexpectedly unfolded. She had woken up in what appeared to be Meligorn but it also seemed so earthly and grounded.

"Oh, look, you decided not to die on me," a familiar voice said before a giggle sounded from the doorway.

All the muscles in Stephanie's body relaxed and the held breath expelled as her eyes focused in on Ms. Elizabeth, who sauntered into the room. "You're here... Man, am I confused."

The ambassador chuckled, walked in behind Elizabeth, and stopped beside the bed. "That is to be expected."

She smiled gently and jolted when her gaze fell to his stomach. He patted his waist and shook his head. "Your magic healed me. And I think you took a few pounds off my waistline. We'd better not tell my wife, though. She might request your services."

Elizabeth snorted. "You go in as a human witch, get in one

battle, and come out as a weight-loss specialist. Only in NorAm. Seriously."

Stephanie leaned back against the headboard. "How are Lars and Marcus?"

The ambassador sat on the edge of the bed and turned toward her. "Like new. Not a trace of pain, no issues, and all their scans came back like nothing ever happened. But you need to stop worrying about everyone else and focus on you."

For the first time since even before the party, Stephanie's thoughts explored her own body. She could feel the exhaustion in every part of her, although it was better than it had been when she last remembered being awake in Lars's lap.

Her gaze drifted to the cracked windows through which the sound of birds chirping lightened the room. "Are we on Meligorn?"

The ambassador looked around and his sigh was almost a laugh. "No. It's merely some magic I put on the place. I figured it would be nicer than you waking up in one of the rooms in our suite in DC. You needed to come back gently and I know how gentle Meligorn can be, especially to someone who loves it as much as you do."

Elizabeth sat down on the other side of her. "You can't stop being a hero, can you?"

Stephanie shrugged. "What can I say? In all honesty, I feel like I have very little in me. My energy is so low I can barely sit here."

The ambassador took her hand and turned it over, then traced his finger over her palm as he whispered words in Meligornian. His eyes flashed a simmering purple and he placed her hand back on her lap. "You are improving but it might take a while. You see, the amount of magic you consumed and pushed out was more than you should have been able to survive. Because of that, it forced open areas of your psyche that humans don't normally ever experience. It isn't a common occurrence on Meligorn, but it has happened enough for us to know about it."

She looked down at her hands, her forehead creased. "Will I recover from it?"

V'ritan nodded. "Yes, of course you will. You are already on your way, although you will have different abilities after this. You unlocked things that weren't really meant to be unlocked, but it has not killed you and I can predict that it will only continue to make you stronger."

"It was Earth energy, wasn't it?" she asked.

The ambassador thought about it for a moment. "I believe that it was. I knew you were full of gifts when I met you but until last night, I had not realized that you have a different flavor of MU. And, in time, I would like to know more about it. These things, in humans, are rare and often so different that we do not have the chance to study them or understand them. I would like to be able to create an understanding of it so that if another reaches a level like this, they will have resources. Understandings. They will not be forced to learn as they go and find themselves in this place or worse. But in the end, it will be up to you what you share with the world. It is your gift."

Stephanie nodded. "Right now, I simply want to get better. I want to be able to work again, function again, and maybe take a walk instead of feeling so tired—and not mentally but physically."

V'ritan patted her on the arm. "You will get there. It has only been a day. Think of how you will feel in five or six."

Elizabeth patted her leg. "You have to learn to take care of yourself first. Because if you crumble, every life you would have touched will crumble too. And we kind of like having you around—when you don't fall into some emo dramatic mode doing katas at six am and never socializing. We weren't fond of that version."

She laughed and focused on the blanket she rubbed between her fingers. "Sorry about that. I guess I let my guilt get the best of me, but I felt so bad for Frog getting so hurt. I didn't know what else to do except start protecting everyone. I realize now, though, that it's a family thing. A team thing. We share in it together—the losses and the victories."

The ambassador nodded and looked into her eyes. "What you have to remember is that you cannot escape loss. It is part of every life. Whether you are Dreth, human, Meligornian, or some species we have yet to encounter, there is loss. The important thing, as I have learned through personal experiences, is how you handle it and walk with that loss and grief that will define the kind of leader and challenger you will become. And you can lean on the ones whom you love. Don't let them get away from you because you are scared."

Elizabeth furrowed her brow and nudged Stephanie. "Yeah. You can't kick their butts one day and ghost them the next. It's not nice. Not that it would affect how those fools feel about you. They went from taking a protection gig to following a leader who touched them to their cores. That is something to be proud of. Something to fight for."

Stephanie smirked in embarrassment. "I was fairly emotional. Although I'm sure that if you told my parents that, they would think you had the wrong girl. The magic made me do it."

The other woman rolled her eyes. "Not an excuse. Oh! And speaking of your parents, we called them and let them know what happened. Apparently, they watched the entire thing live via a feed from a journalist above us. They were terrified when they watched you carried out. Anyway, they are on their way here now. I sent them some first-class TRAM tickets and they boarded this morning. They should arrive soon. I sent Lars to meet them."

Tears welled in Stephanie's eyes. She hadn't realized how much she missed them until that moment. But before she could get too excited, worry settled painfully in her chest. "Wait, what about the new contract they got with the building? They haven't hired a full staff for that yet. They can't give that up for me. I will be fine."

Elizabeth gripped her arm. "Take a deep breath and relax. You were broadcast all over the world. Mr. Martelle called your parents as soon as he had seen the footage of you saving lives. He knew you were connected to them somehow, but until that moment, he did not know you were their daughter. He was very impressed and apparently asked if there was anything you couldn't do."

Stephanie grinned. "I wish the answer to that was yes, but alas, I can do anything."

The older woman raised an eyebrow and looked at V'ritan. "Yeah, she'll be up in no time. The cockiness is already starting to take over again."

He laughed. "She has a pass. I think she has proven that she is…what do humans say? Uhm…rotten ass?"

Both women burst into laughter and Stephanie clutched her side in pain. "Oh. That is the best Meligornian translation fail I have ever heard."

She patted his arm. "It's badass. Not rotten ass. That implies a whole slew of other things that I don't think you and I are quite on the level of friendship to discuss yet."

The ambassador laughed loudly and held his stomach. "Oh, no. I'm so sorry. Right. You have proven to be a badass."

Elizabeth rubbed her face. "You guys will be the death of me. Oh, so anyway, Mr. Martelle told them he wouldn't dock them for wanting to see the Hero of DC. If he could, he would have been on a plane here too."

Stephanie's eyes widened and she shook her head wildly. "Oh, Lord. I mean, that is very nice but how weird would it have been if I had woken up in a castle room, not knowing where I was, and have Mr. Martelle walk in the door? I might have chopped him in the throat or something."

V'ritan shrugged. "Who knows, he might have loved you even more for that."

They all laughed, and Stephanie giggled once again as she

pushed the hair behind her ear. "So, when do I get to go back to my room and the pod and stuff?"

Elizabeth glanced at V'ritan and pressed her lips together. "Well, we've talked about all that with the ambassador. Now, of course, you can decide anything you want, but he believes that it would be better if you stayed here for a while. He is the only one who is equipped to manage what has happened to you. We all came to that agreement, but it is your choice. Still, we hope you stay and let him work with you to help you heal."

Stephanie bit the inside of her cheek. "What exactly are you treating?"

He rubbed his chin. "Let's see…how do I put this? Your channels are ripped wide open and although they may never close, I am the only one on Earth equipped to help you move through that difficult time. It might be challenging. It might not, but it is safer to be near someone who has knowledge of it. At least in my opinion."

Elizabeth leaned forward intently. "And if you are concerned because your security team will be gone, or me, or any of those things, don't be. If you stay, the security team stays, and I stay as well. The ambassador has been kind enough to put us all up so we can help you heal better and can all understand what is happening."

Stephanie's eyes flashed. "Really? You'll all stay?"

"Yep. All of us. And I'm sure your boss will even call to harass you here. We told you that we are now a team, and we would be a really shitty team if you got hurt and we were like, peace out, kiddo. You jump, we jump."

Stephanie felt really special, like all the conversations of being different added up to something she should have realized all along. She was different, but that didn't mean she was alone. That simply means that she had to be different with other people there to care for her. And that was a really great feeling. The loneliness she had created, she had manifested within herself. No one did that to her. No one forced that on her.

"Knock, knock," Lars said and poked his head around the corner. "Oh, hey there, sunshine."

She waved at him. "Hey. Are you feeling okay?"

He scoffed. "Heck yeah. Like a new man. How about you?"

Stephanie shrugged. "Better than I was."

Lars grinned. "Well, I brought something that might make that even better."

He pulled the door open and her mom walked in, dropped her bag, and flung her arms out. The ambassador moved aside to make space for her. "Oh, sweetie. You look so pretty in this gown...and your hair..."

She glanced down and noticed something familiar about the long white nightgown and her hair loosely braided to the side. A little bemused, she turned to the left and looked at her reflection in the mirror on the wall. Beautiful pink and blue flowers seemed almost sewn into her braid and she looked like she had in her dream.

Her mom touched her chin. "What is it, honey?"

There had already been far too many strange occurrences already and she didn't want to tell them, not yet. "Nothing. I'm just so happy to see you."

"How about me, kiddo?" her dad said and opened his arms.

Stephanie laughed as he strode toward her, leaned over, and kissed her on the top of the head. "I missed you too, Dad. You didn't have to break from work to come all the way out here. I'll be okay. I feel terrible."

Her mom slapped her hand gently. "Stop that right now. We are your family. We love you and when you go through it, we go through it too. It sounds so silly but it's true. We can't let you be here without knowing how much we love you."

Her dad set his chin on top of her mom's head. "And Todd sends his love too. He wanted to be here but school and his new military stuff made that impossible. We told him it would be fine. He said he will email you a bunch of his top-pick movies so if you get bored…"

Stephanie's cheeks flushed and she shook her head. "He is a mess. But tell him I miss him too."

Her mom looked around the room, her mental wheels turning. "This room is beautiful, but I have to admit, it looks nothing like the rest of the place."

The girl's eyes widened in excitement. She pulled herself up and turned to dangle her feet off the bed. The ambassador stood and retrieved a set of deep purple robes—again, like her dream. She turned, pulled them on, and adjusted them gently over her shoulders before she grabbed her mom's and dad's hands and took them to the window.

Both their mouths dropped. "So obviously, we aren't really in Meligorn, but we're not in a pod either. The ambassador has put a magic spell on my room. So, when I am here, it looks like a castle bedroom. It's comforting and warm and I feel really good here. But, since you've never been there and the pods aren't your thing, I figured this would be an experience for you."

Cindy laughed and drew her daughter close. "Our lives have been an experience since the day you were born. An adventure that has taken us down some very interesting and strange roads. But just like this spectacular view of Meligorn, every single moment of it has been worth it."

Stephanie tightened her grasp on her father's arm as a wave of dizziness swept over her. The ambassador walked up to her, pressed his thumb to her forehead, and closed his eyes. "Yes, you have done the limit. It's time to lay down for a bit. We'll see how you feel later and maybe you can go for a walk. Right now, though, I would like to steal your father."

She narrowed her eyes. "Why?"

Her father walked her to the bed and popped in front of her vision. "'Cause it's none of your business, woman!"

"Okay, okay." She burst into giggles and waved him off. "Go do what you're going to do then."

The two of them left the room and Cindy sat on the end of the bed next to Elizabeth. They all sat quietly for several moments. Suddenly, the bed shook, and Stephanie laughed herself almost into a crying fit.

The other two women exchanged glances. "What's up?" her mom asked

Stephanie had rolled into bellows of mirth. She shook her head and took a minute to regain her composure. "I just realized Dad went off with the highest ambassador in Meligorn. The next thing that will happen is either a planetary emergency, or they will call that chicken place Dad likes so much—Chicken Palace—to see what it would take to put one on Meligorn."

Elizabeth wrinkled her nose. "I will be brutally honest here, I hope it's that he started an interstellar incident. That chicken is terrifying."

From the hallway, all you could hear was laughter.

CHAPTER TWENTY-FIVE

Stephanie gripped the edges of the wooden podium where she stood on a stage in the conference room of the ambassador's building. She kept her gaze locked on the floor in front of her and fought the exhaustion from the trip downstairs. When she tapped her feet on the floor of the stage, the hollow repercussion vibrated through her. She tugged on the bottom of her Pac Man T-shirt and noticed that her jeans were looser than normal. After four days of rest, which she had definitely needed, she finally accepted that addressing the world had waited long enough.

She looked to where her team stood with Brilgus. Lars and Marcus both raised their hands slowly, kept them close to their bodies, and jokingly gave her the finger. She smirked and tried to hold back the laughter. Brilgus gave her a sweet smile and Elizabeth two thumbs-up. Having them there had already calmed her nerves a fair amount.

Her parents had left the day before. They hadn't wanted to go but had to get back to the business. Stephanie understood that they couldn't give up everything because she went a little wild with her magic. She would talk to them on video chat and she was sure her mom would bug Elizabeth to death making sure she was okay. As for the rest of the guys, they were splitting time between taking care of Frog as he healed at the compound and staying at the ambassador's place to provide protection—and, most importantly, laughs and ridiculous antics that made Brilgus nuts but Stephanie feel right at home.

The Federation Media lead walked up on the stage and leaned toward her. "Whenever you are ready. When you're done, I'll scoot up and take care of the rest. We have a few people talking after you."

Stephanie nodded in understanding and waited for him to walk behind her to where the two navy officers sat as well as the chief of the Federation Police. The crowd grew quiet and Stephanie lifted her chin slowly. A furious flurry of clicks distracted her for a moment as the media snapped as many pictures of her as they could. This was the first time she'd shown her face in public since the incident. Several journal bots buzzed above and made flybys to take pictures of her.

She raised her hands to grip the edges of the podium. A million tact size microphones were placed on the podium in front of her and one larger one for the speaker system in-house. She leaned toward the big one and paused as feedback buzzed in the speakers.

Stephanie had always hated public speaking. "Hi. As most of you know, my name is Stephanie Morgana and I am a human with magical powers. They have asked me to come out today to clear up a few things so that the public can understand my place in the events. It is true that I knew the ambassador for weeks before I acted as his liaison that night. However, I am not—nor do I plan to be—his permanent liaison. On the night of the incident, about an hour before the opening of the gala, I received a phone call from Mr. Brilgus, the ambassador's head of security. I was asked to do a favor for the ambassador and fill in as his liaison for the night due to the fact that the current liaison had gone missing."

She cleared her throat and took a sip of water from the glass on the podium. "I know that Chief Rogers, head of the Federation Police, will talk to you more about the missing liaison. However, we have recently learned, through the exceptional detective work of the department, that the young woman was abducted in order to have someone from inside of their organization fill in at the gala. The ambassador, having keen instincts, found the last-minute change suspicious and therefore denied their replacement and brought me in."

"I want to make this very clear." She took another sip of water and leaned forward slightly on the podium to emphasize the point. "It was purely happenstantial that I was there when all this happened. I was not even on the guest list before filling in that night."

One of the reporters shouted out from the front. "But did you know there was a possible security risk?"

Stephanie shook her head. "No. Two of my personal security team came along only because it was so last-minute. Due to the emergence of my magic, I have been under some scrutiny from certain public entities. I therefore have my own security team to ensure my safety. They worked alongside the brave and heroic members of the Secret Service who lost their lives during this battle."

Another reporter shouted, "How did you do magic like that without a battery? We all saw you drop it on the stairs."

She glanced quickly at Elizabeth, who winked and smiled at her. Slightly uncomfortable, she focused on the reporter who had asked the question. "At this time, I will not discuss the specifics of my personal magical abilities or how they work. Obviously, you can understand that as the only person with these abilities on Earth thus far, I still have many questions of my own. I am sure that when the secret has been fully revealed, it will be shared with you as well."

A couple more shouted and someone snapped another picture, this time with a flash which surprised her. Stephanie squinted and raised her hand. The media lead walked up and leaned into the mic. "As of right now, please hold your questions until the end of the conference. Ms. Morgana is out here voluntarily so that she may be as transparent as possible while providing only facts. We don't want to speculate on anything right now."

He nodded at her and she straightened and gripped the podium, her knees suddenly weak. Lars's face sobered and he stepped forward, about to come on the stage. She put her hand up to stop him and pulled herself upright. Taking a deep breath, she centered herself again.

The reporters had quieted, and the bots hovered at the back. "The other question that I continue to hear on an hourly basis is what happened to me? Everyone witnessed the healing and then my collapse. I can definitively tell you that the magic expulsion during the battle affected my brain. I'm told by those familiar with the phenomenon that I have opened a valley in my psyche, and until I have healed and grown enough to draw the energy required to restore that, I will need a whole lot of rest. That is where I have been for the last four days under the careful watch of the ambassador, my security team, my family, and my manager, Ms. Elizabeth. The ambassador has opened his residence to us, treated us beyond well, and has taken an interest in making sure that I am able to function while I heal."

She cleared her throat again, took another sip, and closed her eyes for a moment so the dizziness could pass. "That is all the information I can give you at this time. The chief and others will come up shortly and they may be able to answer your questions further. But before I leave, I would like to say one more thing. To the people who fought with us, I thank you. For those who gave their lives for us, I thank your families and send you as much love as I have to give. And for everyone else, we are all one species here on Earth. No matter the class, financial status, or job status, we are all the same. So next time you walk around and you see someone who may have older clothes or less of an education or an inferior job, remember that you are no better than them. And if we all start to treat each other equally, maybe changes can begin to take place."

Before anyone could respond, she raised her hand and nodded. "All right, thank you."

Stephanie turned and made her way to the stairs. She held Lars's arm as they walked out of the conference room and down to the elevators. Stephanie grasped him tightly as the doors opened and they stepped inside. As soon as the doors closed, she released a deep breath and her knees buckled. Lars caught her immediately, scooped her up, and held her firmly against him. She was so exhausted. So very exhausted, and all she could do was rest.

Elizabeth closed the door to her room and held her cellphone against her chest. She peeked out the window and into the bathroom before she sat in her chair and drew her knees to her chest. Stephanie had been put back into bed, and Lars remained at her side, taking the first shift to make sure she was not only safe but that she didn't need anything in the meantime.

As she had walked back to her room, her phone had rung. It was Burt and he had a barrage of questions. She now raised her chin and shook her hair back before she lifted the phone to her ear. "Okay, I'm in a better place to talk."

BURT wasn't computing. He couldn't because he had no data on the situation. "I need her to get into a pod. I need it to be her pod."

Her nostrils flared and she lowered her voice. "I am very aware of what you want, Burt, but not everything can jump when you need it to. I am in a difficult situation at the moment. Stephanie is ill, and though she gets a little better every day, she needs someone who understands what's going on to monitor her. That is where the ambassador came into play. He has heard of this happening and knows how to handle it."

"And he can't do that in her own place of residence?" BURT asked, unable to understand the logic. Computing it brought a whole different set of actions.

Elizabeth rolled her eyes and leaned her elbow on the back of the chair as she turned to the side. "I'm sure he could have but he is a busy Meligornian. We can't expect him to come to the compound every day. It was his requirement that if he were to be the one to help her through this, we stay here until she is better. That she does not go home, she doesn't go out, and she stays in her room until this situation is resolved."

BURT began to connect small dots. "That is why you, and most of the security team, have moved in there."

She nodded. "Yes. My requirement was that if she wanted to stay, that me and the rest of the security stay too. We wouldn't simply leave her here. That would have been terrifying for her. And yes, I want to keep my eye on her as well."

He needed her information—a source of growing irritation and frustration—but his system was not currently able to compute an acceptable solution to the predicament. "I don't mind her staying there but I can't check her out without her getting into the pod."

Elizabeth shrugged. "Then I guess we will have to wait. I don't know what else to do. A Meligornian might be her only salvation right now."

Brilgus pushed the start button on the dishwasher and used the dishrag to dry his hands off. It was a lot of work to cook and clean for that many people, but if it helped Stephanie, he would do what was needed. He had never heard of what happened to her, but then again, he might not have ever had a chance to. The rumors were true. He was half and half, one of the very few Meligornian humans he knew of. So, gifts were different with him, and his knowledge of Meligorn had been very limited until he had met the ambassador.

He had spent most of his youth on Earth, while his father, a Meligornian teacher, came back and forth as often as he could. His father had been a good friend of the ambassador's and when he died, V'ritan had taken him under his wing. Brilgus went with what he knew, and he knew that at that point, Stephanie needed rest, close friends and family, and for the rest of the world to leave her alone.

At a loud knock on the front door, he groaned and rolled his eyes. "This is the third time these boys have left their key behind. I'll tape it to their hands next time."

He grabbed the handle and flung the door open, about to say something smart, but stopped at the sight of Federation Military standing at the entrance. "Good afternoon. My name is Corporal Host and we are here on behalf of the Federation Military. We need to speak to Ms. Morgana if she has a minute."

Brilgus shook his head. "I'm sorry but she's resting. Can I ask what this is about?"

The corporal maintained an expressionless face. "Merely some…stuff. It is her business."

This was not looking good in the least.